Railroad Robbery

The paymaster and the paycar guard sat rigid in chairs; two men stood with guns trained on them. Two more men were squatting beside an open safe, transferring its contents to a canvas sack. Slade's voice rang out—

"Elevate! You're covered! In the name of the law—"

The men at the safe leaped erect, while the other two whirled to face Slade. The car rocked to a bellow of gunfire.

Weaving, ducking, slithering, Slade shot with both hands. A slug gashed the flesh of his arm, another tore through the leg of his overalls. One of the robbers slumped to the floor. A second rocked on his heels and fell backward. The two remaining trained their guns on the moving Ranger.

Other *Leisure* books by Bradford Scott:

THE COWPUNCHER
LONGHORN EMPIRE
PANHANDLE PIONEER
TEXAS RANGER
TERROR STALKS THE BORDER

Range Ghost

Bradford Scott

LEISURE BOOKS NEW YORK CITY

A LEISURE BOOK®

February 2010

Published by special arrangement with Golden West Literary Agency.

Dorchester Publishing Co., Inc.
200 Madison Avenue
New York, NY 10016

ISBN 10: 0-8439-6279-8
ISBN 13: 978-0-8439-6279-6
E-ISBN: 978-1-4285-0815-6

The name "Leisure Books" and the stylized "L" with design are trademarks of Dorchester Publishing Co., Inc.

Printed in the United States of America.

10 9 8 7 6 5 4 3 2 1

Visit us online at www.dorchesterpub.com.

Range Ghost

Chapter One

Ranger Walt Slade, named by the *peones* of the Rio Grande River villages *El Halcon*—The Hawk—rode into Amarillo to the not inappropriate rumble of distant thunder. Not too distant, at that, Slade decided as a forked streak of fire split the lowering heavens and was followed by a staccato boom.

He glanced upward as he rode on between two rows of buffalo-hide huts, a remnant of the original Ragtown, as Amarillo was first called.

"We'd better get under cover as quick as we can, Shadow," he told his magnificent black horse. "Otherwise you're liable to get a bath you don't hanker for. Let's go! Just a little ways and around a corner and we'll come to the stable where you hung your hat the last time we were here. Hope there's room, for it's okay and so is the crusty old gent who runs it. Then I'll head for Swivel-eye Sanders' Trail End saloon and a surrounding; been a long time since breakfast, and not much of a breakfast at that. Let's go!"

Shadow snorted cheerful agreement to all that was said and ambled on.

Again a zigzag flash of lightning, and again a roll of thunder—and almost instantly it was echoed by another "thunder," a low-down thunder that could only come from the muzzle of a six-shooter; the sound seemed to come from around the next corner.

"Now what?" Slade wondered as he reined Shadow in, close to one of the buffalo-hide walls.

The report was followed almost instantly by a chatter of hoofs and a volley of angry yells.

Around the corner bulged a horseman, leaning low in the saddle; and he had a gun in his hand. Seeing Slade almost barring his way, he threw up the gun to line sights. For a moment it looked like El Halcon was in for trouble.

However, the horseman had not counted on "the fastest and most accurate gunhand in the whole blasted Southwest!" Slade drew and shot. The rider gave a howl of pain and wrung his blood-spurting hand. The gun spun through the air and hit the ground a dozen feet distant. The fellow reeled in the saddle but kept his seat and went scudding out onto the open prairie.

Slade did not fire a second time, for he didn't know what it was all about and had no desire to kill anybody if he didn't have to.

Again a clatter of hoofs. Around the corner swept half a dozen riders, shouting and cursing. Slade tensed for eventualities.

"Which way did the blankety-blank go?" howled a voice. Slade nodded toward the prairie, where the first rider was in plain sight and going like the wind.

"We'll get him!" yelped the voice and the troop swept past El Halcon without giving him a second glance.

Slade didn't think they would, for the fugitive was well mounted on a tall bay that gave the appearance of speed and endurance, and unless all signs failed, a real Panhandle drencher was going to cut loose at any second, the deluge of rain hiding the pursued like a drawn curtain.

Cries and curses were still sounding beyond the corner. Slade spoke to Shadow,

"Let's see what's going on, feller." The big black moved forward.

Rounding the corner, Slade came upon a group of men bunched about a man stretched on the ground, groaning. The whole front and left side of his shirt was drenched with blood.

El Halcon took in the situation at a glance. He dismounted with lithe grace, flipped open a saddle pouch and from it took a roll of bandage and a jar of antiseptic salve.

"Out of my way!" he said. It was a voice that expected, and got instant obedience. Kneeling beside the injured man he deftly cut away the blood-soaked shirt, exposing the wound, which was bleeding copiously.

"Lie still," he told the man. "That bleeding's got to be stopped." He probed the area of the bullet hole with sensitive fingers.

"High up and through the shoulder, no bones broken so far as I can ascertain," he said. "Lie still."

Swiftly and deftly, he smeared the wound with the salve and padded and bandaged it, curbing the flow of blood.

"Make a pillow for his head from a coat or something," he ordered over his shoulder. "And have a slicker ready to cover him if the rain starts, which it is liable to do any minute. I don't want him moved till the doctor sees him. How do you feel now?"

"A helluva sight better," rumbled the sufferer. "I reckon you saved me from bleeding to death."

"Possibly," Slade conceded. "At least you would have lost a lot more than you should."

For the first time he found time to really look at the wounded man. He was large, bulky, with grizzled hair, a big-featured face and keen blue eyes now slightly filmed with pain. Then with a nod Slade stood up and swept the suddenly silent group with his cold, pale eyes.

"Well, what was it all about?" he asked. "Speak up, somebody."

A lean and wizened individual stepped forward. "Him and Clyde Brent had a falling out," he said in a piping voice.

"I gather he fell out with somebody, but why, and who is Clyde Brent?" Slade countered.

"Brent's the hellion who shot him," said the lean man. "They reached and—"

"Tell him the straight of it, Unger," rumbled up from the ground. "I reached first, but it didn't do me any good. Brent's almighty fast on the draw."

"Not too fast," Slade observed dryly. "But why were you on the prod against each other?"

"Brent runs sheep," broke in the man Unger, his voice almost a snarl.

Slade's eyes seemed to grow a shade colder. "That so?" he said. "And since when is running sheep a capital offense in Potter County? Must have been some changes since I was here last."

With that bleak stare hard on his face, Unger squirmed. "This is cow country," he said, sudenly defensive.

"It was sheep country before it became cattle country," Slade reminded. "And it looks to me like you gentlemen are taking the law in your own hands, which isn't good. Also, odds of six to one are a bit lopsided. Seems that was how many were chasing the man you call Brent."

"Maybe the boys will catch the horned toad," came hopefully from the oldster on the ground.

"I doubt it," Slade said. "He was pulling away

from them, and he appeared to know exactly where he was heading; they may find they have bitten off more than they can comfortably chew."

"That's right," agreed the old man. "Brent has a salty bunch riding for him."

"Owlhoots always have tough jiggers riding for them," Unger put in.

Again Slade let his eyes rest on the other's face. "Have you proof that Brent is an outlaw?" he asked. Unger reluctantly shook his head.

"Guess nobody's proved anything against him, so far," he admitted.

"Then don't go making accusations you can't back up," Slade advised.

"Feller," said Unger, "we seem to be just getting nowhere. I ain't even thanked you for looking after the Boss like you did. I'm Si Unger, range boss for the Diamond F spread. The feller you just took care of is John Fletcher, the owner."

Fletcher raised a rather shaky, big, and gnarled paw. "Guess I'm a lot beholdin' to you, son," he said. "I didn't catch your handle." Slade supplied it and they shook hands.

"And if ever the time comes when I can do something for you, ask darn fast," Fletcher added. "All right, Si, tell him about it."

"Well, it was like this—" Unger began, when there was an interruption.

"Here comes Doc Beard!" somebody shouted.

The old frontier practitioner strode up to the group, lifted an inquiring eyebrow at Slade, who nodded slightly.

"How are you, Walt?" he said. "Why did you plug that old shorthorn? Not that he hasn't had one coming for quite a while."

"He didn't plug me, he patched me up," rumbled Fletcher. "If I'd had to wait for a cross between a mud turtle and a spavined snail like you to get here, I'd have bled to death."

Beard gazed at the blood-soaked remnants of Fletcher's shirt. "Yes, I've a notion you would have," he said soberly. "But if Slade took care of you, I reckon you're okay except for a sore shoulder for a couple of weeks."

Kneeling beside Fletcher, he examined Slade's handiwork and nodded. "Yes, you'll do," he said. "All right, lift him up and get him inside; it's starting to rain. Sure you can have a drink, a dozen of them if you want. Maybe they'll kill you, but I reckon that's too much to ask of even the rotgut they sell in that rumhole across the street. Rustle him a shirt, somebody."

Waving aside assistance, Slade gently raised Fletcher to his feet. He clung to the Ranger with his good hand for a moment, until he was steady. With a hand under his elbow, Slade guided him across to the saloon and deposited him in a chair.

"See you a little later," he promised. "Got to take care of my horse before the rain really gets going. Yes, I know where there's a stable—it's close to here. I'll see you shortly, too," he promised the doctor.

At that moment a man came running in holding a sixgun. "Say," he exclaimed, "ain't this one of Clyde Brent's ivory-handled irons? I picked it up around the corner; got blood on it."

Unger stared at Slade. "By gosh, I rec'lect I did hear a shot around the corner right after Brent hightailed," he said. "Was so bothered about the Boss I forgot all about it. Did you shoot that hogleg outa Brent's hand, Slade?"

"I did," El Halcon replied.

"Out of his hand on purpose?" Unger asked incredulously.

"Yes," Slade answered. "I had no desire to kill him, not knowing what it was all about and giving an excited man the benefit of the doubt, but when he lined sights with me I figured I'd better prevent him from doing something he'd probably have been sorry for later."

"Shot it outa his hand when he had the pull on you," Unger said in awed tones. "The chance you took!"

"Wasn't much of a chance," Slade deprecated the feat. "He was slow as cold molasses and he throws up instead of shooting straight from the hip."

Unger shook his head and whistled, while Fletcher stared and blinked.

"Clyde Brent slow!" said the range boss. "Gentlemen, hush!"

Slade smiled, and left the saloon.

"Shot the gun outa Clyde Brent's hand!" Unger repeated dazedly.

Old Doc, taking his cue from Slade's slight nod when they met beside the wounded Fletcher, decided it was a good time to drop his bombshell.

"Guess it wasn't much of a trick for El Halcon," he observed casually. His hearers regarded him wide-eyed.

"El Halcon!" repeated Unger. "By gosh, Doc, you're right. Now I've got him placed. I never saw him before but I heard folks talking about what he looked like. And that black horse! Say, he was the feller who killed Veck Sosna, the big he-wolf of the Comanchero outlaw pack, ain't that right?"

"Guess so," admitted Doc.

"And Slade really killed him!"

"Well, if he didn't a coupla fellers with shovels played a mighty mean trick on Sosna," Doc said dryly. "Yep, Sosna's planted up on Boothill. Or what the worms have left of him. Slade chased him all over Texas and Mexico, with Sosna just slipping out of the loop a few times. But Slade finally caught up with him here in Amarillo, and Sosna got his comeuppance. Yep, he's El Halcon. 'The singingest man in the whole Southwest, with the fastest gunhand!'"

"Heard some folks say he's just an owlhoot himself," a voice remarked.

"The world's fulla damn fools!" roared John Fletcher, glaring about like an angry lion. "Who's the skunk who said that?" Unger dropped a hand to his gun-butt.

Nobody admitted ownership.

"Waiter!" bawled Fletcher, "bring everybody a snort. An owlhoot! The blankety-blank-blanks!"

"Rec'lect hearing he palled around with Sheriff Carter when he was here before, worked with him some," observed Unger. "And Brian Carter don't take up with no owlhoots."

Owing to his habit of working under cover as much as possible, and often not revealing his Ranger connections, Walt Slade had acquired a peculiar dual reputation. Those who knew the truth swore that he was not only the most fearless but the ablest of the Rangers. Others, who knew him only as El Halcon, were wont to declare he was just another blasted owlhoot too smart to get caught, so far, but who would get his comeuppance sooner or later. Still others who also knew him only as El Halcon vigorously defended him. "Killings to his credit? You're darn right to his credit! Ever hear of him killing anybody who hadn't one coming and overdue? A chore for the duly elected or appointed peace officers, eh? Well, when the peace officers can't make the grade, they're darn glad to have El Halcon lend a helping hand." And so the argument raged.

The deception, which Slade did nothing to correct, worried Captain Jim McNelty, the famous Commander of the Border Battalion of the Texas Rangers, who feared his Lieutenant and ace-man might come to harm at the hands of some trigger-quick deputy or marshal, to say nothing of professional gunslingers out to enhance their reputation by downing the notorious El Halcon, and not above shooting in the back to achieve their aims. However, Slade would point out—

"Folks will talk in my presence who wouldn't talk in the presence of a known Ranger. And outlaws, considering me just one of their own brand, sometimes get a mite careless."

So Captain Jim would grumble, but not specifically forbid the deception. And Slade would chuckle, and blithely amble along as El Halcon and bother about the future and its possible hazards not at all.

And the Mexican *peones* and other humble people would say, "El Halcon! the just, the good, the friend of the lowly. *El Dios*, guard him!"—which Slade considered the finest compliment he could receive.

At times Slade was inclined to wonder if he hadn't developed a sort of dual personality, too. For it appeared that in moments of stress or peril, "El Halcon," the great mountain hawk with its telescopic eyes, amazingly keen ears, and hair-trigger perceptions gained the ascendancy and dominated his thought and action.

He was inclined to scoff at such a patent absurdity,

but after all, he was descended in part from the wild Highlanders of the Scottish glens, who firmly believed in such things as the second sight which enabled one to, dimly at least, forecast the future and govern one's self accordingly.

All theory, nothing more, of course, but all progress was based on theory, imagination and—dreams.

At the stable, the old keeper greeted Slade warmly. "And the cayuse remembers me," he chuckled, greatly pleased, and reached out a fearless hand, into which Shadow thrust his velvety muzzle, blowing softly through his nose.

"First time you were here you had to introduce me before he'd let me touch him," he continued. "Guess he'd have taken off half my arm if you hadn't. He's a one-man horse, all right, the sort I like. He'll get the best."

Confident that Shadow would lack for nothing, Slade donned his slicker, for now it was really raining, and repaired to a hotel on Tyler Street he had patronized before and registered for a room, in which he stowed his saddle pouches. Then he returned to the saloon. Old John, fortified by a couple of snorts, was feeling much better.

"Sit down and have a snort with us, have a dozen," he boomed.

"I'll settle for one, and then something to eat," Slade accepted, doffing his hat and slicker and drawing up a chair. "Beginning to feel a mite lank."

Meanwhile the old stable keeper was having a talk with Shadow. "Yep, you're just about the finest cayuse I ever laid eyes on," he said as he busied himself with currycomb and brush. "And the feller who forks you is one of the finest looking men I ever saw. A big feller, too. Big with the sorta bigness that is real bigness and not just overpacking of tallow. Yep, he sure is."

The keeper was right. Walt Slade was very tall, more than six feet, and the breadth of his shoulders and the depth of his chest slimming down to a sinewy waist were in keeping with his splendid height. A rather wide mouth, grin-quirked at the corners, relieved somewhat the tinge of fierceness evinced by the prominent hawk nose above and the powerful jaw and chin beneath. His lean cheeks were deeply bronzed. His thick, crisp hair was the same color as the "midnight-black" of Shadow's glossy coat.

The sternly handsome countenance was dominated by long, black-lashed eyes of very pale gray—cold, reckless eyes that nevertheless seemed to have little devils of laughter dancing in their clear depths. Devils that, should occasion warrant, could be anything but laughing.

His dress was that of the rangeland—bibless overalls, soft blue shirt with vivid neckerchief looped at the throat, well-scuffed half-boots of softly tanned leather, and broad-brimmed "J.B.," the rainshed of the cowhand—and he wore it with the same careless grace with which he would wear evening clothes. Around his waist were double cartridge belts from the carefully worked and oiled cut-out holsters of which protruded the plain black butts of heavy guns, from which his slender, powerful hands seemed never far away.

All in all, he looked to be a better outfitted and more than average prosperous chuck-line riding cowhand, which was what he wished to look.

"Pretty good chuck served here," said Fletcher. "We usually eat at Swivel-eye Sanders' place, the Trail End, but this joint ain't so bad—a new one. Tore down some of the hide shacks and put in a decent building, like they're doing all over town. This pueblo is growing."

"It is," Slade agreed, sipping his drink. "A lot of new construction since I was here last year, decidedly noticeable."

"Yep, she's growing," Fletcher said, adding confidently, "We've got no local government, so far, and the county officials sorta run things and try to keep down trouble. Yep, she's growing. Going to take over the Cowboy Capital from Tascosa, which is sure on the wane. I figure Amarillo will be the real city of the Panhandle country before she's finished."

Slade thought so, too, and future events would justify his faith in the town that later would be called the Queen City of the Texas Panhandle, that vast plains empire which would be famous not only for cattle and sheep but for agricultural products, oil, gas, and helium as well.

Right now, however, Amarillo was strictly a Border boom town and made hell-raising a specialty, having also usurped that prerogative from Tascosa in the Canadian River Valley.

Not that Tascosa was dead yet—far from it—but, as Fletcher said, it was on the wane. The hoped-for Rock Island Railroad had bypassed the former Cowboy Capital, fifty miles to the north, and the great ranches, such as the XIT—"Ten Counties in Texas"—land donated in payment for the construction of the State capitol building, had fenced off the trail herds coming up from the south, which had been Tascosa's life blood.

Yes, Tascosa was on the wane, while Amarillo was on the boom. With two railroads, it was now the shipping point for the herds from the south.

While Slade was eating, the Diamond F hands filed in from their fruitless chase of Clyde Brent, drenched, disgruntled, and worried about Fletcher. However, their apprehensions on his account were quickly relieved and Unger gave them a vivid account of the happenings in their absence, ending dramatically with—

"Yep, we now have El Halcon in our midst, praise be!"

The hands stared, almost in awe, at the man whose exploits were fast becoming legendary throughout the Southwest. All insisted on shaking hands and thanking him for looking after Fletcher.

"We'd hate to lose him," said one. "He's such a prime example of what an owner shouldn't be."

"Uh-huh, and if you did lose me, you'd starve to death," the rancher retorted. "Nobody else would be loco enough to hire you."

"Glad to hear you admit you're loco, we've knowed it for a long time," said the speaker, a gray-haired, wrinkle-faced oldtimer.

"Oh, sit down and shut up!" snorted Fletcher. "Your tongue goes like a dry wind mill, and just sucks air. So Brent got away from you, eh?"

"Yep," said the other as he drew up a chair. "Left us standin' still, and then down came the rain. I've a notion that bay of his is just about the finest cayuse in this section."

"Not quite," differed Unger, glancing at Slade.

"But we'll drop a loop on the hellion yet," declared the oldtimer.

Fletcher shook his head decidedly. "Nope," he said, "Slade says to let him alone, so let him alone."

"But what if him and his horned toads jump us?" protested the other.

"I somehow doubt if they will," Slade said. "Of course, if you are attacked, you have a right to defend yourselves, but don't start anything."

The hands didn't look particularly pleased with the prospect, but after a glance at him proferred no argument and got busy on their food and drinks.

"Here comes the sheriff," somebody remarked. "Thought he'd show up soon as he got back in town."

Big and bulky old Sheriff Brian Carter approached the table and surveyed its occupants with little favor.

"All right," he said, "let's have it; what happened?"

Unger repeated the story for his benefit. The sheriff glowered at Slade.

"Might have knowed it," he snorted. "Trouble! Trouble! Trouble! Just nacherly follows you around and starts soon as you show up. Ain't I got enough troubles without you? How are you, Walt? Glad to see you still kicking and out of jail." He shook hands with vigor, sat down and accepted a drink.

After a bit, Slade pushed back his empty plate and rolled a cigarette.

"Another snort?" Fletcher suggested.

"I think I'll make out with another cup of coffee," El Halcon replied.

"Waiter!" bawled Fletcher.

Doc Beard shoved aside his glass. "Let's have another look at that shoulder, John," he siad.

Fletcher doffed his borrowed shirt. Doc opened his bag and swiftly changed the pad and bandage.

"That'll hold you," he said. "Bleeding's stopped, and it's a clean hole without any damaged bones. Guess you'd better spend the night in town, though; no sense in taking a chance of starting the bleeding again."

"Figured on staying in anyhow," replied Fletcher. "Payday, you know, and the hellions have to have their bust."

"Maybe they'll bust their blasted necks 'fore the night's over," Doc said hopefully as he closed the bag. "Guess I'll amble over to my office and get ready for plenty of business, what with its being payday and El Halcon being here, too. Be seeing you."

"They don't come any better," Fletcher remarked, followed the old doctor's progress to the door with his eyes. "Knows his business, too. Say, the rain's stopped and the sun's beginning to shine. Looks like it'll be a nice night, after all."

The low-lying sun was indeed flooding the prairie with reddish light. A little breeze shook down showers of fiery gems from the grass heads. Outside sounded the clump of hoofs on the muddy street. The hands from the nearer ranches were already riding in for the bust. Soon Amarillo would begin to howl.

Slade's pulses quickened. Young, vigorous, filled with lusty life, he was forced to admit he liked such nights with their promise of entertainment and excitement—sometimes just a mite too much excitement for peaceful comfort. Well, that was all part of the game, and welcome. Soon he'd get the lowdown from Sheriff Carter concerning the recent goings-on which were the reason for his being in Amarillo a little sooner than he had expected to again visit the Cowboy Capital.

Fletcher was speaking. "Suppose we amble over to Swivel-eye Sanders' Trail End?" he suggested. "Be folks we know there. Coming along, Slade?"

El Halcon glanced at the sheriff, who nodded. "Be seeing you there later," he said.

After the bunch had ambled out, Slade turned to

the sheriff. "How about going to your office where
we can talk uninterrupted?" he said.

"That's a notion," Carter agreed, rising to his feet.
"No tab—Fletcher took care of everything."

Reaching the small building which housed the office, they mounted a couple of steps onto a little covered porch that canopied the door. Carter unlocked it
and they entered, closing the door behind them. The
sheriff drew a shade over the single window and lit
the lamp, for the sun had set and it was growing
dusky. They sat down with their chairs comfortably
tilted back against the wall.

"Brian, just what's going on hereabouts?" Slade
asked.

"Walt, there's plenty," the sheriff replied. "Never
seen anything like it."

"So I gathered from your letter to McNelty," Slade
said. "But what specifically?"

"Well," answered Carter, "the Tascosa stage was
robbed of a hefty money shipment. A feller who runs
a sort of bank for cowhands up at Gluck was murdered and robbed. A saloon right here in Amarillo,
down by the lake, was robbed, a bartender killed.
Two cowhands were found murdered down there,
their pockets emptied. There's been cow stealing
right and left. It's not only here in Potter County but
in Oldham and Hartley as well. A bunch of hellions
'pear to be swallerforkin' all over the section. Nobody knows who they are or where they come from;
I figure they have their headquarters here in Amarillo, but I could be wrong about that. Getting so
everybody is looking sideways at everybody else.
The oldtimers are getting together and the newcomers
are sorta bunchin'. We could have a range war on

our hands to liven up things still more. Nobody seems safe. Even the big spreads like the Frying Pan have been losing stock, to say nothing of the smaller ones up to the north and over to the east. It's bad."

"So it seems," Slade admitted soberly. "What about the row between Fletcher and Clyde Brent?"

"That one could really end up blowin' things wide open," replied Carter. "Brent is one of the newcomers, been here less than a year, and Fletcher is one of the real oldtimers. Brent's holding, which ain't very big, is up to the northeast, butts against the Canadian River Valley. Fletcher's is west of Brent's. It's a big one. Brent has sorta newfangled notions. Been running in something he calls improved stock."

"Something all cowmen will have to do if they hope to survive," Slade interpolated. "The market for longhorns is closing out; people are demanding better beef than the longhorns supply. Go ahead."

"Well, Fletcher didn't like it, especially after Brent began stringing barbed wire." Slade interrupted again.

"Something else the oldtimers have got to get used to. For a long time the really big fellows like the XIT have strung wire. Open range will not be able to compete with fenced pasture."

"That's right," Carter admitted. "But up to the east and the north is still open range, with fellers like Fletcher against wire."

"How about Brent's sheep?"

"You know how the oldtimers feel about sheep," Carter countered. "Even when they're fenced in they are suspicious of them. Say it's just a matter of time till they're turned loose to ruin range. Hard to make them believe anything else."

"Does Brent keep his woolies fenced in?"

"He does," the sheriff had to admit. "He's got some broken ground on the north of his holding. No good for cows but all right for sheep. He says sheep will tide a feller over when the cow market is bad for a time."

"And he's right," Slade said. "So it boils down to Fletcher being on the prod against Brent because he ran in sheep and is a newcomer?"

"Guess that's about it," the sheriff conceded. "But that's enough to stir up real trouble between them and always liable to suck others into the row, on one side or the other."

"I think," Slade said, "that I have slowed that one up to an extent; I practically secured a promise from Fletcher and his hands not to start anything with Brent."

"Well, that helps," replied Carter. "Now if you can just manage to get the same sort of a promise from Brent. Afraid he don't feel over kind toward you right now, though, after you knocked a hunk of meat outa his hand."

"I've a notion he'll cool down, after his hand stops smarting, and if he is at all fair-minded he will realize that he made a mistake in throwing down on me like he did and forced me to do what I did for my own protection."

"Oh, I expect he'll figure he made a mistake, all right," Carter agreed dryly. "He's lucky you didn't take him a mite more seriously or he might have made a worse mistake."

Slade smiled, and changed the subject. "So it looks like we have our work cut out for us," he observed. "Well, I'll scout around a bit and try and learn something. I am inclined to say it is not a unique situation, typical of the new lawless element invading the West; just as salty as the oldtimers but with more brains. And you have no notion as to who might be heading the organization? No suspects?"

The sheriff shook his head. "Not a darn one I can really call a suspect," he admitted. "That's the worst of it. When you were here before and chasin' your Veck Sosna, you at least knew who to look for."

"Yes, that was an advantage," Slade agreed. "Well, we'll see what we shall see."

"And meanwhile, keep your eyes skun and watch your step," cautioned the sheriff. "Mighty apt to be certain hellions around who don't care much for you, and the word El Halcon is in town will get around mighty fast."

"I'll be careful," Slade promised carelessly.

Carter stuffed tobacco into his pipe, Slade rolled a cigarette and they sat smoking in silence, each busy with his own thoughts.

Abruptly, Slade raised his head in an attitude of listening. His unusually keen ears had caught a sound, a tiny metallic sound that seemed to come from the front door, as if a cautious hand had touched the knob. Another moment and he heard another sound, equally tiny but different, a faint wooden creaking— such a sound as would be made by a foot pressing a slightly loose floor board. Seemed almost as if someone had approached the door, then stealthily retreated.

Instantly "El Halcon," sensitive to anything out of the ordinary or not immediately explainable, was in the ascendancy. Slade listened a moment more, then noiselessly rose to his feet, motioning the sheriff to stay where he was. Gliding across the room, he seized the door knob and by almost imperceptible degrees turned it. Standing well to one side, with a quick jerk he flung the door wide open.

There was a booming explosion. Buckshot screeched through the opening and splattered the far wall.

Chapter Two

Slade went backward in a cat-like leap, a gun in each hand, his eyes fixed on the open door, through which drifted smoke rings. Nothing happened. He cast a swift look out the door; there was nobody in sight. Gliding forward again, he glanced up and down the street. Still nobody in sight; but there was a corner only a few yards distant. He holstered his guns and stepped out the door onto the porch.

The sheriff was raving profanity. "What the blankety-blank blue blazes!" he stormed.

"Looks like you were right when you said the word El Halcon is in town would get around fast. Take a look," Slade replied.

Sheriff Carter, gripping his gun butt, glared at the contraption roped to one of the porch posts, a sawed-off shotgun, its double muzzles trained on the door. He outdid his former efforts at swearing.

"If we'd opened the door to go out, we'd have gotten those blue whistlers dead center!" he bawled.

"Yes, there would have been enough to take care of both of us," Slade agreed cheerfully as he cut the cords that held the shotgun to the post. From the triggers dangled a broken wire, the far end of which hung from the door knob.

"How in blazes did you catch on?" demanded Carter.

"When the sidewinder looped the wire over the knob he touched the knob and it rattled," Slade explained. "Then when he slid off the porch he stepped on a loose board and it creaked. I thought it sounded a little funny and decided a mite of investigation was in order."

"Thank Pete you did!" growled the sheriff, wiping his moist brow. "The nerve of that hellion, shootin' up the sheriff's office!"

"Yes, plenty of savvy, and plenty of cold nerve," Slade agreed. "Just luck he didn't get away with it."

"Luck!" snorted Carter. "I call it something else. Blazes! I got the shakes. Of all the things for anybody to do!"

"Yes, it was a mite original," Slade agreed. "I very nearly ran into a somewhat similar scheme once, a scattergun set up inside a room, but this is different and most unexpected. You plumb sure Veck Sosna was dead when you buried him? Looks exactly like one of his capers."

"Well, he sure didn't climb up the handle of the spade," replied Carter. "Hope there hasn't another of his caliber coiled his twine hereabouts, but I'm hanged if it don't look like there has."

"Let's get inside," Slade suggested. "I see some folks coming up the street; they may have heard the reports and are trying to locate where they came from. Best to keep what happened under our hats—may tend to puzzle the hellions responsible."

Reentering the office, they closed the door. A moment later they heard the voices of the passers-by, receding into the distance.

"Chances are they'll figure it was just some cowhands skylarking, which is to be expected on payday night," Slade said. He passed the shotgun to the sheriff.

"Lock it up," he directed. "A nice souvenir for you."

"I can do without such souvenirs," Carter growled as he slammed the sawed-off in a desk drawer and turned the key. "Might turn out to be evidence of some sort, though."

"Doubtful, but it might," Slade conceded. "Well, suppose we drop over to the Trail End; I can stand a cup of coffee about now."

"And I can stand a coupla dozen snorts," growled the sheriff. "I still got the shakes. Let's go!"

When they entered the Trail End, big, burly, and bony Swivel-eye Sanders, the owner, came hurrying foward with hand outstretched.

"Mr. Slade!" he exclaimed. "Heard you were coming in and have been waiting for you. Come along, Mr. Fletcher has saved a couple of chairs at his table for you fellers. Said you should be along soon. I'll rustle some drinks."

There was no doubt, Slade thought, but that Swivel-eye came rightly by his peculiar nickname. His eyes did seem to swivel in every direction. One eyelid hung continually lower than the other and viewed from a certain angle lent his otherwise rather saturnine face an air of droll and unexpected waggery; he seemed to glower with one eye and leer jocosely with the other. One profile appeared jovial, the other sinister. A sudden full-face and the viewer was bewildered and didn't know just what conclusion to arrive at. However, he had a well-shaped mouth and a good nose, and Slade knew him to be a square shooter and dependable.

Fletcher, already well fortified, whooped a greeting. "Not much past dark and things are beginning to hop," he said. "Shoulder? Don't hurt a bit, thanks to Slade and old Doc. Guess it was shock more than anything else that sorta knocked me out for a spell.

Anyhow, I feel fine now. Here comes Swivel-eye with drinks; that'll help."

Sipping his drink, and ordering coffee with which to wash it down, Slade glanced about the Trail End, a typical cow-town saloon only bigger and better appointed than most. There was the usual long bar, a dance floor, roulette wheels, a faro bank, poker tables, and others for diners who preferred leisurely eating to grabbing a snack at the spotlessly clean lunch counter.

Fletcher downed his drink and said, "I'm going over to the bar with the boys for a little while. You sticking around, Slade?"

"Yes, for a while, anyhow," the Ranger replied. "Later I figure to amble about town for a bit. Want to drop down to the lake and see Thankful Yates at his Washout saloon."

"That rumhole!" growled the sheriff. "Always something happening thereabouts. Ain't safe to be alive down there."

"But interesting," Slade replied. "I found it quite so the last time I was here."

"That time you had Jerry Norman, old Keith Norman's niece with you," the sheriff pointed out. "As you said, she's a good luck piece."

"She sure was that day in the Canadian Valley when the drygulchers jumped us," Slade said. "If she hadn't downed the one who was lining sights with me, I wouldn't be here talking about it."

"She's a real gal, all right," said Carter. "Hope you get to see her this trip."

"I'm sure going to try to," Slade replied.

He was destined to, sooner than he expected.

The sheriff went back to the former subject under discussion—

"I can't get over the nerve of that wind spider, riggin' up that infernal contraption to the post outside, where anybody passin' by could see him working at it."

"Not much traffic on that side street, and it was quite dark," Slade pointed out. "He worked smooth, all right, didn't make a sound roping the scattergun to the post. If he hadn't touched the door knob when he looped the wire over it, he might well have been successful."

"And if it wasn't for you having ears like nobody else has, he *would* have gotten by with it," Carter declared. "I didn't hear a thing."

"Perhaps you weren't listening close," Slade smiled. The sheriff snorted, and called for another drink. Slade settled for a cup of coffee. After finishing it, he glanced around the room, which was crowded, noisy, but to all appearances harmless enough, so far.

"Brian," he said, "I'm going to walk down to the Washout; will be back soon."

"Okay," replied Carter. "Only be careful, it's a rough section."

"I will," Slade promised and left the saloon.

The walk to the Washout was uneventful. When he arrived there, Thankful Yates, big, burly, and fiercely mustached as before, spotted him at once and came hurrying with outstretched hand.

"Mr. Slade!" he exclaimed. "Well, well, it's fine to see you again. Wait just a minute till I tie onto a bottle of my private stock." He hustled to the back room.

Glancing about, Slade's attention centered on a group of half a dozen or so cowhands standing at the bar who were regarding him intently. As Yates departed, one, a hulking fellow with bristling red hair and truculent eyes, detached himself from the group and swaggered toward Slade, pausing a few feet distant and looking him up and down.

"Guess you're the feller I'm looking for," he said.

"Yes?" Slade replied, his voice deceptively mild. Thankful Yates, who was approaching with a bottle, made no move to interfere. Only he stared hard at the other cowhands and nodded significantly toward the bar, behind which his head drink juggler stood with a sawed-off shotgun ready for business.

"Yes," said the redhead. "Guess you're the feller who shot the boss in the hand, ain't you?"

"Possibly," Slade conceded, his voice still mild.

"Guess hitting him in the hand was sorta accident, eh?" said the big fellow.

"I don't think so," Slade replied.

"I figure it was," said the redhead, scowling ferociously. "And I figure you ain't as good as folks say you are." He dropped a hand to his gun butt. Thankful Yates chuckled softly. Slade made no move.

"Go ahead and pull it," he said.

The big fellow tried to—and looked into two rock-steady black muzzles that yawned hungrily toward him. And back of those muzz'es were the terrible eyes of El Halcon!

"Still think it was an accident?" Slade asked softly.

The other gaped and blanched. "I—I—" he began dazedly. A voice interrupted—

"Crowly! What the devil are you trying to do, get yourself killed?"

The speaker was a freckle-faced young fellow sitting at a nearby table, his bandaged right hand resting on the tab'e top.

"I—I figured he was overrated," Crowly gulped.

"Well, I reckon now you know better," said the other. "Behave yourself while you're still in one piece."

Stifling a grin, Slade holstered his guns with the same blinding speed with which he had drawn them, turned his back on the dazed Crowly and approached the table.

"Sorry I had to do it, Mr. Brent," he said, glancing at the bandaged hand, "but you didn't give me much choice."

"Oh, forget it," said Brent. "I was wrong, but I thought you were another of those Diamond F hellions. Sit down, won't you?"

Thankful Yates, making no mention of what for a moment had looked like grim drama in the making but which had quickly deteriorated to a farce, filled glasses with great deliberation, and one for himself.

"Mr. Slade only drinks my private stock," he observed. He grinned at Crowly. "Guess you'd better have one, too, Pete. You 'pear to need it."

Crowly, who looked like a man who had just glanced across into eternity and saw it wasn't far, nodded his bristly head. "I need a dozen," he mumbled. "Much obliged, Yates." Brent grinned also and regarded Slade.

"Mighty glad you dropped in when you did," he said. "We came down here so there'd be less chance of running into the Diamond F bunch; I'm not looking for trouble."

"They're up at the Trail End," Slade replied, sipping his glass. "And I think it would be a good idea for you to come along with me and shake hands with Fletcher."

"Huh!" gurgled Brent, very nearly choking over his drink. "Do you mean it?"

"I do," Slade answered. "Fletcher promised me he wouldn't start trouble with you fellows. He meant it. Yes, I think it would be a good idea for you follows to get together and let bygones be bygones. What do you say? Bring your bunch along with you if you wish to."

"Well, if you say it's so, I guess it is," sighed Brent. "All right, we'll take a chance, just as soon as we finish our drinks."

He joined his hands at the bar and began speaking to them. They looked a bit startled, but nodded agreement. Slade turned to Yates.

"I'll be back," he said. A few moments later, with Brent on one side and big Crowly on the other, the hands trailing behind, he led the way from the Washout and uptown to the Trail End.

When Slade arrived at Trail End with his slightly apprehensive entourage, there were stares a-plenty. Old John Fletcher gulped and goggled, but when Slade said, "Mr. Fletcher, Mr. Brent would like to shake hands with you and forget the past," he didn't hesitate, but thrust out his big paw.

"Okay, Brent," he said. "Let's see if we can't make a go of it from now on. Might as well. There's no arg'fyin' with *him!* Just gets you nowhere. Have a drink, all of you."

When Slade entered the Trail End, sweeping the room with his glance, as usual, he saw a face he instantly recognized. Seated alone at a table was a modishly dressed young lady. She was a rather small girl with great dark eyes, very red lips, and dark hair inclined to curl. Her figure left nothing to be desired.

With a word to Fletcher, Slade strode across to her table. "Jerry!" he exclaimed.

The girl, whose attention appeared fixed on the bar, or its occupants, turned her head.

"Good evening, Mr. Slade," she said coolly, and turned back toward the bar.

Chapter Three

Somewhat taken aback by the casual greeting, Slade stared at her. For a moment he seemed at a loss for words, something quite unusual for El Halcon. He tried a jocular remark—

"Looking for your gentleman friend?"

"Which one?" she asked, without turning her head. Again the normally poised and thoroughly self-sufficient Ranger appeared somewhat off balance. And he experienced a sense of irritation. Or was it wounded vanity? His black brows drew together and he regarded her in silence, with the sense of irritation or whatever the devil it was completely taking over.

"Sorry to have intruded," he said stiffly, and half turned to go, failing to note the slyly sideways glint of the big eyes.

Suddenly she laughed—a gay, ringing laugh, her little teeth flashing white against the scarlet of her lips.

"Don't look so put out, my dear," she said. "I saw your name on the hotel register and just thought I'd have a little fun. Sit down, darling, and don't mind me."

"Jerry Norman," he replied, "you are a devil!"

"Uh-huh, but you used to say I was a nice devil," she said.

"And I still say it," he answered, "but you've got the sense of humor of an imp!" He sat down and gazed appreciatively at her elfinly beautiful little heart-shaped face.

"So you did come back!" she voiced the obvious.

"Didn't I tell you I would?" he countered.

"Yes, but of course I didn't believe you. Or at least that it would be so soon, with all the stops you must have had to make."

"Stops?"

"Of course. How are all your women?"

"Women!" He endeavored to look indignantly innocent, and failed signally. Jerry giggled and regarded him with dancing eyes.

"Oh, I don't mind, too much," she said. "I think I'd worry more if there were only one; then you might get really interested in her."

"It's just possible that I am really interested in only one," he replied with a meaningful glance.

"Perhaps," she conceded, her beautiful eyes suddenly slightly wistful, "but remember the last lines of your song—I'll never forget them—

> *'But oh, the wind upon the trail!*
> *And the dust of gypsy feet!'*

"As I said once before, the wind and the dust and the gypsy trails—those are the real rivals."

Walt Slade was silent.

Very quickly she was gay and laughing once more. "Uncle Keith was overjoyed when he saw your name on the register and knew you were in town, and so were the boys, and old Pedro, the cook, of course," she said.

"I'll be glad to see all of them, and it's wonderful to see you again," he replied.

"Nice of you to say it," she said. "And are you going to take me down to that lovely place, the Washout, again, and that nice Mr. Yates?"

"I've a notion that adjective has never before been applied to the Washout," he answered. "But Thankful Yates is nice. Yes, I'll take you, if you really wish to go. Don't forget, things were a bit rough the last time we were there."

"And I liked it, even though I was scared stiff for a minute," she said. "Soon as I saw you were all right, I really enjoyed the excitement."

"Yes, I think you did," he replied. "But remember what the sheriff said—flying lead plays no favorites."

"And perhaps you'll remember that flying lead doesn't frighten me to an extent I don't know what's the right thing to do," she countered.

"Yes, I remember," he admitted soberly. "I'm not likely to forget it."

"Uncle Keith and the boys will be here after a while," she said. "They stopped at a place on Filmore Street, where they have some friends. We don't have to wait for them, though; we'll see them later."

Slade glanced toward the bar, where old John Fletcher and Clyde Brent, glasses in hand, were conversing animatedly, the two outfits mingling.

At the moment, Sheriff Carter entered. He stared at the group at the bar and shook his head resignedly.

"So you did it again," he said accusingly to Slade as he drew up a chair and sat down. "Hello, Jerry. As usual, the young hellion made peace between a couple of outfits on the prod against each other. I don't know how the devil he does it, but he does."

"Yes, he always makes everybody do just what he wants them to do," answered Jerry.

"Perhaps," Slade put in, "it's just that I sort of provide them with an opportunity to do what they really wanted to do all along, if they could just dig up an excuse for doing it. Right, Jerry?"

Miss Norman wrinkled her pert nose at him and did not deign to reply.

"I just came up from the Washout," Carter commented reflectively. "Yates told me what you did to Pete Crowly; sure took him down a peg. He holds his comb pretty high when it comes to handling a gun, and he's a trouble hunter. Brent usually manages to keep him fairly well in line, but now and then he kicks over the traces, or tries to. Guess he's still trying to figure out just what happened."

"How was that?" Jerry asked.

Carter told her, in detail. She shook her curly head and sighed.

"Yes, I guess Pete learned a lesson, too," she said.

"Uh-huh, and one I figure he won't forget soon," said the sheriff. "May do him good to know there's better men in the world than him."

"I've a notion he's not a bad fellow, down at the bottom," Slade observed.

"Maybe so, but if so, it's way down," said Carter. "And here comes another one I've been keepin' an eye on."

The newcomer was a big man, almost as big as Crowly, and had something of the same irascible countenance. His eyes were quick and bright and moving, sweeping the room with their glance. Shouldering his way rather roughly to the bar, he ordered a drink and, Slade thought, continued to survey the room in the backbar mirror.

"Why, it's Neale Ditmar, our new neighbor on the east," Jerry said.

"Uh-huh, and I wish he'd stayed a lot farther east," grumbled Carter. "He's another trouble hunter or I'm a heap mistook. Ugly customer in a rough-and-tumble, I gather. Had a ruckus with a couple fellers in one of those rumholes down by the lake and cleaned 'em both. One he had on the floor pulled a gun, but Ditmark kicked it outa his hand, busted a couple of fingers, I heard."

"What was the row about?" Slade asked, mildly curious.

"Oh, over a dance-floor gal, I believe," replied the sherfiff. "Or some similar sorta trifle."

"Well! I like that," said Jerry. "So a woman is just a trifle and not worth fighting for, eh?"

"I didn't say that," the sheriff protested. "I meant the ruckus was just a trifle."

Miss Norman sniffed delicately and crinkled her eyes at Slade.

"Been quite a few changes since you were here last, Walt," she said. "We've got a new neighbor to the west, too. A Mr. Tobar Shaw, a very pleasant person and gentlemanly. He bought the Hartsook place. Calvin Hartsook was murdered by wideloopers about five months back. His daughter was his only heir and she's married to a bank clerk in Dallas who knows nothing about ranching and, I understand, cares less. So they put the spread up for sale at a low price and Mr. Shaw bought it. It isn't very big but good grass, and he's been running in some improved stock, almost as good as ours. I've a notion he'll make a go of it. Appears to favor progressive methods."

"Yes, Shaw seems to be all right," put in Carter. "I've talked with him a couple of times. A notion you'd like him, Walt. I figure he's a sorta educated feller."

Slade nodded without speaking; he was studying Neale Ditmar's profile and broad back. He experienced a feeling that Mr. Ditmar was a mite out of the ordinary.

Jerry jumped to her feet. "Come on, Walt, take me to the Washout," she said. "It's nice here, but too quiet."

The sheriff wagged disapprovingly. "Everybody to their taste, as the herder said when he kissed the sheep. Hope you don't get walloped by a thrown bottle or something."

"I'll chance it," Jerry replied cheerfully. "Come on, Walt, Uncle Keith will take care of the check; he'll feel bad if he isn't allowed to. Be seeing you, Uncle Brian.

"This is better," she said, snuggling closer as they turned into a quiet and fairly dark side street, and raising her face.

"And *that's* a lot better," she added, a moment later, when her lips were free for speaking. "I was beginning to wonder if you were ever going to—again."

The Washout was not quiet, far from it. Jerry's eyes were sparkling as they made their way to a table near the dance floor, which at the moment happened to be vacant. "There's Mr. Yates, he's seen us."

Old Thankful came hurrying forward, bottles in hand. "Well! well!" he exclaimed. "Miss Norman again; she hasn't been here since you brought her the last time, Mr. Slade."

"As I told you before, Uncle Keith won't take me to the really interesting places," Jerry replied, extending her little sun-golden hand. "How are you, Mr. Yates? It's good to see you again."

"And it's plumb wonderful to see you again," Thankful said gallantly. "Here's your favorite wine.

See, I didn't forget. And a snort from my private bottle for Mr. Slade before he starts in on coffee."

He filled glasses to the brim, chuckled, and hurried back to the far end of the bar, where his head drink juggler was making need-of-help motions.

"Even more crowded, busier and noisier than the last time we were here," Slade remarked. "Quite a few people from uptown, in addition to the cowhands. Well, he runs a square place, and the word gets around."

"And it seems everybody is in town tonight," Jerry observed, gazing toward the bar. "There's our other new neighbor, Mr. Shaw. The tall man with the yellow hair." Slade regarded him with interest.

Unlike Neale Ditmar, who exuded personality, Tobar Shaw was not a man to catch the eye and hold it. In appearance and dress he differed little from any other fairly well-to-do rancher. He was mildly handsome, Slade thought, with his yellow hair inclined to curl, a broad forehead and deep-set eyes; at that distance, Slade could not ascertain their color. In build he was tall and lean but broad-shouldered.

At that moment, Shaw turned toward the table, nodded genially to Jerry and walked to the far end of the bar, where he engaged Thankful Yates in conversation. Jerry was speaking and Slade forgot all about him.

"Here come Uncle Keith and the boys!" she exclaimed. "Looking for us, I expect. You remember the boys, of course—Joyce Echols and Cale Fenton you kept from being murdered by the Sosna rustlers, and Bolivar, the range boss, and old Pedro, the cook, and the others. Look at them sift sand!"

The XT bunch came plowing through the crowd, whooping joyously at sight of Slade. After a gabble of conversation and hand-shaking all around, the hands trooped to the bar. Old Keith Norman drew up a chair and ordered drinks for everybody.

"See there's our new neighbor, Tobar Shaw, talking with Thankful," he remarked. Catching the rancher's eye, he waved a cordial greeting, which Shaw returned.

"Guess Jerry told you about him and Neale Ditmar, eh?" Norman went on. "Shaw kept the old Hartsook brand, the Bradded H, but Ditmar changed his and uses a Tumbling D burn. Shaw 'pears to be a nice friendly feller, but Ditmar is sorta uppity. Civil enough, but carries his comb sorta high. Oh, well, we're getting all kinds. Funny, ain't it, new folks coming in from every direction, but a lot of the old-timers are pulling out, like Webb, who sold to Ditmar. Some of 'em say it's getting too dadblamed crowded hereabouts and are heading for New Mexico and Arizona. Up at Tascosa, they're leaving like fleas from a singed coyote's back."

Norman paused to take a drink, and then resumed, "Others say they just can't make a go of it against the widelooping we've been having during the past few months; it's bad. The way things are going, it begins to look like that soon there won't be any real old fellers here 'cept John Fletcher and me—he don't aim to move come hell and high water, unless he really has to. Saw Fletcher up at the Trail End. He swears you saved his life, and I've a notion you did. He won't forget it. He told me about how you took Pete Crowly down a peg. Like to split my sides laughin' over that one. Figured to pull against El Halcon, eh? Guess he'll know better next time. Crowly's another uppity cuss. I sorta like his boss, young Brent. You sure did a good chore in getting those two outfits together. We were all scairt real trouble would come from their snappin' at each other."

"You have been losing stock, Mr. Norman?" Slade asked.

"Uh-huh, more'n I like to think about," Norman replied.

"Any notion where they run them?"

Norman shrugged. "Guess there's only one way they can run 'em, west by way of the Canadian River Valley," he replied. "But they sure do it slick—nobody's been able to catch 'em up. Sure no running them across the desert to the south of the Canadian, not over that flattened-out streak of hell with no water; no cows could make it."

With which Slade was ready to agree.

"Trouble is, it's just about impossible to track a herd across our range, to the Canadian or anyplace else," Norman added. "The grass jumps right back up after a hoof has pressed it and don't leave any mark at all." He paused for a moment, looking reflective. Slade was again willing to agree with his statement; he recalled what was written by Pedro de Castaneda, Coronado's scrivener, in his journal of that explorer's expedition across the Texas Panhandle:

> "Who would believe that a thousand horses and five hundred of our cows, and more than five thousand rams and ewes, and more than fifteen hundred friendly Indians and servants, in traveling over these plains, would leave no more trace where they had passed than if nothing had been there—nothing—so that it was necessary to make piles of bones and cow dung now and then, so that the rear guard could follow the army. The grass never failed to come erect after it had been trodden down."

Which peculiarity worked in favor of the wide-loopers; tracking them was almost an impossibility. Old Keith was speaking again.

"Funny thing happened," he said. "A bunch of stock was run off from around a waterhole with a little crik running out of it. For some reason or other, along that crik for nearly half a mile the grass is sorta sparse, hardly any at all. My boys who were trying to trail the stock swore that the marks of their hoofs and the horses' irons were plumb plain on that stretch, and that they headed not north to the Canadian, but *south*. That's what they said, south. I told them they were loco, but Joyce Echols said, 'All right, come and see for yourself.'"

"Did you?" Slade asked, abruptly interested.

"I did," Norman admitted. "Hanged if they weren't right. Yes, sir, for a good half mile those darned tracks held south by a mite west. Of course when they hit the tall grass again we lost 'em, but the last we saw of 'em they were sure headed south, never turned."

Slade nodded and did not comment. He had let the garrulous oldtimer run on because he felt he was gathering needed information relative to prevailing conditions. Now he desired time to do a little thinking on what he had learned.

"Like to dance?" he asked Jerry.

"I'd love to," the girl replied. "Floor sure is crowded, but we'll make out."

"Just gives the fellers a chance to hold the gals tighter and the gals don't seem to mind," Norman remarked. "I see Shaw is leaving and Thankful's coming over to talk with me. Go to it! I'll be at the bar when you get back."

The floor was crowded, all right, but that didn't pose much of a problem to such expert dancers as Slade and Jerry Norman. Her cheeks were rosy, her eyes sparkling, and she was a bit breathless when, after several fast numbers, they returned to their table.

"Wonderful!" she exclaimed. "Uncle Keith was right. You held me like—like when—well, you held me! Now I want a glass of wine."

Slade poured it and remarked, "You didn't mention to me that you were losing stock."

"I was so glad to see you I forgot all about it," she replied. "Yes, we have lost quite a few cows, but it's slackened up a bit since we started patrolling the range at night. Mr. Shaw is patrolling, too, and so, I heard, is Ditmar. But somehow they keep slipping bunches through from the spreads north of the Canadian River. I don't know how they do it, but they do."

Slade nodded thoughtfully and let the subject drop for the time being.

Frankly he doubted that the rustlers shoved the stolen cows south and west across the Tucumcari Desert; without water the distance was too great, no herd could make it. He suspected that the tracks Norman saw were in the nature of a blind to foil possible pursuit, the cattle really being turned back to follow the course of the Canadian. Well, perhaps he'd be able to find out about that later; an idea was building up in his mind, something in the nature of his noteworthy "hunches," but an idea. He resolved to pay a visit to the Valley soon.

Chapter Four

Now the Washout was really hopping. Every table was occupied, the bar was crowded three deep. All appeared to be noise and gaiety and in order—in so far as anything serious was concerned. Slade was thoroughly enjoying himself.

Nevertheless, he was growing restless. He felt he was accomplishing nothing, and not likely to so far as the Washout was concerned. He wondered what the street and other places were like.

Young Joyce Echols came over from the bar and asked Jerry to dance.

"I'll look out the door a minute," Slade told her. Jerry understood perfectly what he had in mind, and why, there being no secrets between them. Her eyes were anxious as she accompanied Echols to the dance floor.

The street was just as crowded as the Washout, and just as noisy. But, like in the Washout, everybody appeared cheerful and happy, though apparently imbued by a mounting ambition to get drunk as quickly as possible. It was a typical payday bust in a typical cow town.

For Amarillo was still a cow town despite the steady encroachment of agriculture and sheep. Here still the cowboy was king and the prosperity of the growing town still centered about him. Slade shrewdly surmised that the time was fast approaching when it would be different, when the Queen City of the

Panhandle would owe its phenomenal growth to factors other than cattle. He had a theory relative to as yet little suspected potential wealth in the vicinity, still jealously guarded by inscrutable nature. He wondered if others had an inkling of its existence.

His theory was not mere unsubstantiated theory; there were certain surface indications that were highly significant to the trained engineer with an exhaustive knowledge of geology and petrology, the science of rocks; and Walt Slade was that kind of an engineer.

Shortly before the death of his father, which followed financial reverses that led to the loss of the elder Slade's ranch, young Walt had graduated from a noted college of engineering. He had a postgraduate course in view that would better fit him for the profession he had resolved to make his life's work.

This for the moment was out of the question and Slade was undecided as to just which way to turn. While he was pondering the matter, he visited Captain Jim McNelty and Captain Jim had a suggestion to make that commended itself to Slade.

"Walt," said Captain Jim, "why don't you sign up with the Rangers for a while and pursue your studies in spare time? You seemed to like the work when you served with me some during summer vacations, and I consider you darn good Ranger material."

So instead of a civil engineer, Walt Slade became a Texas Ranger, and almost before he realized it, the short term of service he had planned was jogging along through the years.

For Ranger work had gotten a strong hold on him providing as it did so many opportunities to right wrongs, help deserving people, and make his land a better land. He found he was loath to sever connections with the illustrious body of law-enforcement officers—that was, just yet—plenty of time to be an engineer.

As he strolled along the crowded street, he smiled at recalling the lucrative offers he had received from noted men of finance and industry, such as James G. "Jaggers" Dunn, General Manager of the great C. & P. Railroad System, former governor Jim Hogg, and John Warne "Bet-a-Million" Gates, the Wall Street tycoon. When he would finally decide to resign his Ranger commission, there was little doubt that his future would be assured.

Often his knowledge of engineering and kindred subjects had proven of great help in the course of his Ranger activities. He felt that right here might well be such an instance.

As he drew nearer the lake front, the streets became darker, the racket from the many saloons more raucous. Now El Halcon walked with care, taking note of all things that might be sinister, his gaze probing alley mouths and doorways, scanning passers-by. Frequently he glanced over his shoulder in an effort to ascertain whether he was being followed. That, however, was difficult, for there were quite a few people on the street.

His stroll was not aimless but in line with a definite course of action. He didn't know where to come by the outlaws, so he determined to give the outlaws an opportunity to come to him. If he had been watched in the Washout or elsewhere, such might develop.

That the plan was hazardous, he well know, but being very much on the alert, El Halcon did not give that contingency very serious thought. He had little fear of being taken by surprise and felt able to take care of any happening so long as he was prepared.

So far as he could see, no one gave him a second glance. Everybody appeared intent on his or her business, for here there were women on the streets, dance-floor girls who had slipped out with their partners, and others who had just "slipped out."

He entered one of the dingy saloons and ordered a drink which he sipped slowly, studying the crowd the while. Nobody paid any attention to him; nothing happened. He tried a second with likewise negative results. It began to look like he was pursuing a fruitless quest.

Then in the third place he hit paydirt, and in such an unexpected manner that it very nearly caught El Halcon off balance—very nearly, but not quite.

He was standing at the bar, not far from the door, when the three men entered. The foremost was heavily built and fairly tall. The pair trailing after him were lean, wiry men of slighter build. The big man, after a glance around, walked up to Slade, almost within arm's reach, and halted, a scowl darkening his blocky, bad-tempered face.

"El Halcon, ain't it?" he asked in a gravelly voice that carried to all parts of the room.

"Been called that," Slade admitted, very much on the alert, his attention mostly focused on the pair behind the speaker, who had paused directly back of him.

"We don't want your sort here; this is a law-abiding place," the big man said, raising his voice. "Get out!" As he spoke he slewed sideways from in front of his companions.

Slade hit him, with all his two hundred pounds back of his steely fist. The fellow shot through the air, landed on the floor with a crash, and stayed there. The pair went for their guns.

El Halcon drew, but he did not shoot. With his blinding speed and the pair of killers so close, it wasn't necessary. The heavy barrels of his Colts slashed right and left, and there were three forms on the floor, two of them pouring blood from split scalps.

In the same flicker of movement, Slade whirled toward the crowd, the black muzzles of his guns thrusting to the front.

"Anybody else interested?" he asked. "I aim to accommodate."

There was dead silence. Men stood rigid, careful not to move a hand, lest it be misinterpreted by the grim figure facing them. Slade swept the room with his glance and backed slowly to the door where he paused and holstered his guns, his hands hovering over the black butts. He glanced at the three unconscious forms on the floor—he'd know them did he see them again—and spoke, casually—

"Gentlemen, I think it would be a good idea to stay inside for a while. Otherwise, I *might* get nervous."

Still there was silence. He eased through the door, took two long strides up the street and turned, his eyes on the door. Nobody came out. He turned again and strode on, neither fast nor slow. Another glance back and he turned a corner and continued to the Washout.

It had been a nice try, all right, carefully planned and novel—the big man meant to center his attention for the instant needed by the two gunmen to get into action. And he had provided an "alibi," a justifiable motive for the killing, to protect the community from El Halcon, the notorious outlaw; and they might well have gotten away with it. However, it appeared they were not very familiar with El Halcon, or had perhaps believed him overrated. Well, they quite likely would come back to consciousness with an altered opinion.

He could have killed all three, of course, but he considered he had handled the affair the better way and was very well satisfied with the night's work. Dead men tell no tales, true, but dead men also do not show the way to whoever sends them on their errand. He had not only frustrated another attempt against his life, but he also had three of the outfit spotted, which might be more productive of good results than just doing away with three hired hands.

"Well, couldn't you find her?" Jerry asked.

"Didn't look for her," he replied as he sat down.

"But what if she comes looking for you?"

"Then I'll let you take care of the situation," he countered.

"I will," Miss Norman declared energetically. "I have fingernails."

"That's right, you have," he agreed reminiscently, with a slight twitch of his shoulders. Jerry giggled, and changed the subject.

He did not tell her of the encounter, there being no point in needlessly worrying her. After a bit, Joyce Echols approached and asked her to dance again. While they were on the floor, Sheriff Carter strolled in.

"Well?" he remarked, interrogatively, after he had ordered a snort, and coffee for Slade.

The Ranger related in detail his brush with the three killers. Carter swore with explosive violence.

"That was a new one, all right," he commented. "But I figure the hellions didn't know El Halcon very well or they wouldn't have tried it."

"So I assumed," Slade agreed. "But it may provide

us with a much needed lead. I may get a chance to spot them in somebody's company and eventually get a line on the brains of the outfit. I haven't the slightest notion who he might be or where to look for him, the way the situation stands at present. Well, here's hoping."

"If you can manage to stay alive long enough," the sheriff said morosely. "They sure are after you."

"Which means, I'd say, that they are quite perturbed and may end up doing something rash," Slade predicted.

"Maybe." The sheriff was pessimistic. "I'd say that after what happened tonight they're liable to pull in their horns a little. Two flops in two tries must be a mite discouraging. I've a notion they're still trying to figure how the devil you escaped that shotgun trap set for you at the office. Well, I'll keep an eye out for a coupla busted heads and a swole jaw; guess you gave the hellions something to remember you by, anyhow."

"How are things uptown?" Slade asked. The sheriff shrugged.

"A lot of fuss and noise and general heck-raising, but no real trouble, so far," he replied. "I've got three specials on the job in addition to my three regular deputies, and they are keeping things pretty well under control. Something may cut loose before the night is over, never known it to fail, but the redeye hasn't started to really get in its licks yet. Wait!" Slade was inclined to agree.

The night wore on, with nothing untoward happening. The Washout continued noisy and hilarious, but peaceful enough so far as any real trouble was concerned. Finally old Keith and the XT hands approached Slade's table.

"What you say we amble up to the Trail End for a last snort," he suggested. "Getting late."

"Not a bad notion," Slade agreed. "All set to go, Jerry?"

"I am getting just a wee bit tired," the girl admitted. "So much noise and smoke; but I've enjoyed every minute of it. And for once you didn't get into trouble."

Slade smiled and did not comment. "Let's go," he said.

The Trail End was still fairly lively, but quieting down as tired nature took toll. Norman and the hands lurched to the bar for their snorts. Slade and Jerry had coffee at a table. When the cups were empty, she glanced suggestively at the clock.

"Let's go," Slade repeated. He was watchful in the course of the short walk to the hotel, although he did not really expect any further trouble, and didn't encounter any.

The old desk clerk was to all appearances snugged in dreamland, but he opened one eye and smiled benignly as they mounted the stairs together.

Chapter Five

The XT bunch headed back to their spread shortly after noon the following day.

"Work to do," said old Keith. "That is if the blasted wideloopers have left us anything to work with. Be seeing you, Slade."

"And you'll be out to the place before long, won't you, dear?" Jerry asked.

"Yes, I'll be there shortly," he promised.

"I'll be waiting."

After they rode away, Slade repaired to the sheriff's office for a confab with Carter.

"What's your next move?" said the sheriff.

"I think I'll give the Canadian Valley a once-over," the Ranger decided. "I know some folks there who might be able to give a line on something. Somehow I figure that Valley is the key to the rustling activities, and that it is the same bunch that's been responsible for the robberies and killings that have recently happened."

"And you figure that if you can drop a loop on the rustlers, you'll clean up the whole mess?"

"That's the way I regard it," Slade conceded.

"John Fletcher, a good part of whose holding lies to the north of the Valley, and who has lost a lot of stock, 'lows he believes the hellions do run them by way of the Canadian and not north to Oklahoma as some folks think," the sheriff remarked reflectively.

"He may well be right," Slade replied. "I'm of the

opinion it could be done. Folks who live in the plazas there, mostly Mexicans, are reticent and not
much on talking about what they see, fearing repri-
sals, and if the wideloopers can stay well to the
north when they pass Tascosa they can very likely
make the run without detection or interference. The
run to Oklahoma is a straight one but it has its draw-
backs in that it's vulnerable to pursuit. Flat prairie
and no cover. A stolen herd could be sighted a long
ways."

"Guess that's so," the sheriff agreed. "But sure
looks to me like somebody would sight the devils
making that long run through the valley and across
into New Mexico and the hills. Farther south the hills
are closer."

"But then they would have to cross the desert without water, that is so far as anybody knows. Ranger
Captain Arrington and his men made it across by the
Lost Lakes that were not supposed to exist, but they
entered the desert by way of Gaines County, far to
the south of here. Arrington thought the lake he
named Ranger Lake was in Gaines County, Texas,
but of course we know now that all the lakes are in
New Mexico. However, it would be impossible to run
a stolen herd south through Texas for such a distance
without it being detected. So that route is not to be
considered. If by any chance they do cross the desert
a short distance south of the Valley, there must be
water somewhere about half way across, and so far
there has never been a report of any."

Slade paused for a moment to roll and light a cigarette. His eyes grew thoughtful.

"But the Indians knew things we don't know," he
added. "Perhaps there is hidden water out there

somewhere; it is not beyond the realm of the possible. Nor altogether impossible to discover it, that is, if it really does exist.

"And as I said, there are people in the Valley who will talk to me; they have been of assistance to me before. So I'm going to chance a sashay into the Valley and see if I can't learn something. Doesn't appear to be anything to learn here, at the moment. Be seeing you." With which he headed for Shadow's domicile and got the rig on the big black.

"Time for a little leg-stretching," he said. Shadow snorted cheerful agreement.

Wishing to reach the Valley as quickly as possible, Slade rode almost due north at a good pace. It was a beautiful afternoon, the prairie flooded with golden sunshine, and the air held an autumn crispness. Already the grass heads were turning ameythst and the shallow hollows were bronzed with the fading ferns. The blue bowl of the sky pressed down upon the land in a perfect circle, with the ever retreating horizon holding its perfect curve into infinity, or so it seemed to the horseman who rode across the flat expanse with never a hill or a tree in sight and only the whisper of the wind in the grasses to break the all-pervading silence.

Some fifteen miles to the north of Amarillo, the monotonous expanse was cut by a valley, rough and broken, several hundred feet lower than the plains north and south of it, down which flowed an eccentric river that at times was but a mere trickle, at others a raging flood wallowing over treacherous quicksands. The valley was grown with scrubby cedar and mesquite and bushes and occasional tall trees, and grass that came belly-high on a horse. It was a welcome relief to the endless vista of flatness that hemmed it in on either side.

This was the Canadian Valley, an oasis in a "desert" of grass.

Walt Slade liked the prairie, but he liked the rugged valley better, where grew wild choke berries, plums, wild gooseberries, and grapes, where birds made music in the thickets and little animals went about their various businesses cheerfully and without fear, and the living water made its sprightly song and chuckled to itself over outlandish and doubtless ribald secrets of its own.

The Valley had always attracted "little people" who found food, shelter, and happiness here—which was perhaps why El Halcon liked it so well.

There were ways to enter the Valley with its precipitous sides and walls of rock, some well known, some otherwise. The best known and easiest crossing was where several creeks converged on the north side of the river and there were broad meadows of spring-fed grass. Here for ages the buffaloes and other wild animals crossed to the south plains, pausing to feed on the luxurious grass. The Indians and the white explorers followed their trails.

Here, on the north bank of the bridged Canadian River grew the town of Tascosa, for many years the legendary Cowboy Capital of the Plains, around which was waged the struggle between the "little" men and the cattle kings of the rangeland empire of Texas.

However, Slade's goal was not Tascosa; there he would be able to learn little more than in Amarillo. It was the dwellings of the little men he sought, where he believed he could garner valuable information relative to the widelooping activities in the section.

The Valley was not always peaceful. Here rode the cow thief and the outlaw, and bloody battles were fought amid the cedars and the mesquite.

After the first ten miles, Slade veered a little more to the west and when he reached the Valley he turned due west, riding along the lip of the great trough. He knew of a little-known descent into the Valley that was so hidden by straggles of brush and tall grass as to be almost indiscernible from only a few yards distant. Without mishap he reached the spot and drew rein. For some minutes he sat scanning the prairie in every direction. It stretched lonely and deserted in the redding rays of the low-lying sun.

"Okay, feller, down you go," he told the horse. "You've been here before."

Just as he was about to begin the rather precipitous descent, he reined in again, studying the ground with his keen eyes.

"Darned if it doesn't look like cows have been here, and not so long ago," he remarked. Again he gazed across the rangeland and could discern no clumps of grazing cattle.

Guess they must have wandered off to better feeding grounds," he said. "Let's go!"

With only a protesting snort or two, the big black made it to the Valley floor. Now the sun was low in the west and the great bowl was growing shadowy.

When Slade reached the river, he turned upstream, following its course.

For several miles he rode steadily, with the Valley growing ever more darkening. It was still fairly light, however, when he rounded a bend and came

upon a cleared space where sat a small adobe surrounded by a flourishing garden patch. Nearby
grazed a few sheep and goats. A window glowed
golden.

"Looks like the old gent is still here, all right," he
remarked to Shadow and raised his voice in a shout.

After a moment the door opened and an old Mexican peered out questioningly. He stared, gave a
glad cry and came hurrying forward.

"*Capitan!*" he exclaimed. "Once again you return
to old Estaban! Ha! and the beautiful *caballo!* I he
knows at once. First to the stable, *Capitan,* where with
my mules he partakes of the best. Then, coffee
steams in the pot and meat sizzles in the skillet.
The feast of celebration we shall have, even to the
bottle of golden wine from my own grapes."

With dispatch, Shadow was stalled in the comfortable stable with a pensive mule to keep him company,
his feedbox filled with oats, and shortly afterward
Slade sat down at a table loaded with appetizing food
and drink.

There followed a period that was mostly busy silence. Finally, Slade pushed back his empty plate
with a sigh of content and rolled a cigarette. Estaban
poured a final cup of steaming coffee to go with the
wine and manufactured a husk *cigaro.*

For some minutes they smoked in relaxed and
full-fed comfort. Then Estaban spoke.

"*Capitan,*" he asked, "what seek you? Never do you
ride without a reason."

"Cows," was the laconic reply. "Stolen cows that I
thought may have perhaps come this way."

Estaban shook his head. "No *ganado* have come
this way," he answered, adding, "but they have entered the Valley but recently."

"But if they didn't come this way, where in blazes did they go?" Slade demanded.

"*Capitan,*" said the old Mexican, "came you to the Valley by your usual way?"

"Why, yes," El Halcon replied. "I descended a couple of miles or so to the east, like before."

"Well," said Estaban, "by that way the *ganado* departed from the Valley, as did they who herded them."

Slade stared at him. "I did spot cow tracks on top of the sag, but figured they were left by some grazing critters," he said. "If they left the Valley by way of that crossing, where in blazes did they go from up top the slope?"

Estaban shrugged with Latin eloquence. "*Capitan,* that I do not know. Them I did not follow; it is not discreet to do so."

"Decidedly not," Slade agreed.

"I would presume," added Estaban, "that they continued south. Much unlikely that they would turn east or west."

"Darned unlikely," Slade replied. "Well, this sort of tangles my twine for me. I was sure they would pass up the Valley and on to New Mexico and the hills."

"That they did not," insisted Estaban. "And I have heard that others crossed the Valley to the west of here and reached the outer plains by another little used route up the slope."

"Which means," Slade said slowly, "that they must have finally turned west to the desert. And no herd of beefs could cross that desert without water. A large portion of the first half of the drive would have to be made during the burning daylight hours. By nightfall the cattle would be completely exhausted, would have to be allowed to rest, and without water would perish."

Estaban shrugged again. "*Capitan*, I know not the answer, but pass up the Valley they did not," he declared.

For some minutes Slade sat silent, pondering this most puzzling bit of information. No more than Estaban did he know the answer. He could only conclude that if the widelooped cows were turned west south of the Canadian, there must be water somewhere out on that inferno of heat and sand and alkali dust. He recalled that oldtimers insisted that the Indians did use the desert route to run stock and that they knew where water was to be found—which Slade had always discounted. Explorers had crossed the desert on horseback more than once and all had reported it to be a waterless waste where, should a sudden windstorm arise, and they were frequent, even a man on a good horse took his life in his hands when attempting the crossing.

Well, he had to find the answer somehow. And meanwhile he was evolving a plan that, with a little luck, might be productive of results. It was an exceedingly hazardous plan and a little slip on his part could easily prove fatal. However, he felt the possible gain was worth some risk.

"Estaban," he said, "when did the last bunch cross the Valley, do you know?"

"*Si*," the Mexican replied. "Five nights agone. There are those here who are curious and who, well hidden, have watched. None watch tonight, for it is a night of *fiesta* at the plazas and all attend to take part in the merrymaking."

"Five nights since anything went through," the Ranger repeated thoughtfully. "And last night was the payday bust, with most of the hands from the spreads in town. I know nearly all of John Fletcher's Diamond F bunch were, and tonight they will sleep soundly. Anyhow, I'm going to play a hunch. Yes, I've a notion the gents might try to pull something tonight."

"But why not last night when most of the *vaqueros* were in town getting drunk?" Estaban wondered.

"Because formerly payday night was quite frequently when raids were made, but of late the cattlemen have been taking added precautions on payday nights and have several riders patrolling the range. Whoever is heading the operations in this section has brains and would take that into consideration. Largely guesswork on my part, of course, but worth giving some thought to. Anyhow, I'm going to play the hunch."

"You will be in great danger, *Capitan*, a lone man against many desperate *ladrones*."

"Not too much, if I can work it so the element of surprise is my advantage," Slade answered. "I'll take it easy for a couple more hours and give Shadow a chance to catch his breath and then I'll ride. By that time there will be a moon in the sky, which should help."

"*Capitan*, let me accompany you," said Estaban.

Slade shook his head. "No, I think I can handle this one better by myself. If it comes to a showdown and things get a mite too hot, I always have Shadow to depend on; he can show his heels to anything I'm likely to meet up with. You've already been a great help, providing me with the information I so sorely needed. And you have reversed my deductions as to where they run the cows. How they do it I still don't know, but the knowledge that they do it is highly important. Now I've just got to find out how, which shouldn't be impossible."

"*Vaya usted con Dios*—Go you with God—" Esta-ban said devoutly.

"*Gracias*," Slade replied. "And that helps, too."

Chapter Six

The two hours passed quickly, with the moon climbing higher and higher in the sky. Slade got the rig on Shadow who, filled to the ears with oats, was all set to go. With a *"buenas noches"* to Estaban, El Halcon rode back down the Valley to where the ascent of the south slope was possible.

He rode slowly, for he was confident that nothing would occur until around midnight or even later. Once where the moonlight beat strongly on a stand of cliffs that for a short distance replaced the slopes, he pulled to a halt and sat studying the jagged wall.

"Shadow," he said, "unless I'm greatly mistaken, and I don't think I am, the petrologic outcroppings indicate that the lower slope of this area is not from north to south as generally supposed, but from south to north. From which I'm beginning to develop a theory, a theory I believe will be substantiated by future mineral discoveries in this section. You'll remember I once arrived at a similar conclusion in another part of the country, and that was proven correct by future discoveries. I wonder if somebody else has arrived at a like conclusion here? Interesting."

He rode on, deep in thought, and finally reached the point where an ascent by horses, and cattle, was possible. Turning south, he sent the black up the slope to the crest, where he reined in again and studied the possibilities of the terrain.

Along the lip of the Valley was one of the few

spots where there was some growth encroaching on the plains. Here there was more than average. About three score yards distance from the point of the ascent, a stand of thick and tall chaparral reached out onto the prairie for quite some distance, a hundred feet or more. Slade regarded it with approval.

" 'Pears made to order for us," he told Shadow. "Yep, there's where we'll make our stand."

First of all he moved the horse well away from the lip, where it should be safe from flying lead. At the edge of the growth he flipped out the bit and loosened the cinches a little, so the cayuse would be comfortable.

"Stay there in the dark," he ordered. Shadow blew through his nose and did not commit himself. However, Slade knew he would stay put. Walking back until he was close to the edge of the slope, he eased into the chaparral, leaned against a convenient trunk and rolled and lighted a cigarette without fear of the tiny flare of the match being detected. There was nobody around and he would hear the approaching cattle, did any approach, long before they reached the crest of the ascent.

The hours passed slowly. The great clock in the sky crossed the zenith and wheeled westward, and nothing happened. After another tedious wait, El Halcon began wondering if he was following a cold trail, if his hunch wasn't a straight one, after all. Seemed that if the wideloopers were really active, they should have put in an appearance before now, it being imperative that they have the herd shoved well out onto the desert before daybreak were they to avoid detection.

Then abruptly he heard a sound, thin with distance but without doubt the querulous bleat of an irritated steer. His pulses leaped exultantly; he had guessed right, a stolen bunch was being run across the Valley. He picked up his high-powered Winchester, a "special" procured for him by General Manager Jaggers Dunn, which he had leaned against the tree trunk, and made sure the mechanism was in perfect order. Then, tense and eager, he waited.

Some minutes passed, and again the bleat came, much closer. Another ten minutes and he knew the cows were mounting the slope.

The foremost bulged into view, blowing and snorting, and were followed by more and more. It was a good-sized herd, more than a hundred head, a heavy loss for some owner and a very lucrative haul for the rustlers. Slade moved a little farther to the front, peering through a final straggle of twigs and branches. He raised the rifle.

The sensible thing would have been to open fire as soon as the wideloopers came into view, but he was a Texas Ranger and must give the murderous devils the chance they didn't deserve, even at the risk of his own life.

The last cow scrambled over the lip. Behind it streamed six horsemen. They bunched together for a moment to give the cattle a chance to catch their breath before lining them up in marching order. Slade's voice rang out—

"Elevate! You're covered!"

There was a chorus of startled exclamations, the whitish blur of faces turned toward the sound, then a clutching of weapons. Shots rang out, but Slade had instantly shifted position after speaking and none of the slugs came very close. His eyes, the cold gray of a stormy sky, glanced along the sights.

The Winchester bucked against his shoulder,

spouted flame. A man whirled from the saddle to lie
motionless. Answering bullets stormed past, close,
for he didn't have time to complete his shift. One
ripped his shirt sleeve and just grazed the skin of
his arm. Another shredded his hatbrim. He shot
again, and another saddle was emptied. A slug that
barely touched his temple hurled him sideways
with the shock, which may have been the best thing
that could have happened, for the rustlers fired at
the flash.

A third time the heavy rifle boomed. A third man
reeled and lurched sideways, clutching the saddle
horn for support.

A voice yelled an order. The rustlers, shouting
curses, whirled their mounts and went charging down
the slope to the valley floor, Slade speeding them on
their way with lead until the magazine was empty.
Swiftly he refilled it with fresh cartridges, listening
intently the while against the chance that one might
halt and come creeping back up the slope, hoping to
catch him unawares. But his keen ears told him the
four sets of hoofs kept pounding on after they thudded onto the gorge floor. Evidently the hellions had
all of him they wanted.

With caution he approached the two forms on the
ground but quickly saw there was nothing to fear
from them. By the aid of a match he examined the
dead faces. One he had never seen before, but the
other, big and bulky, with a still somewhat swollen
jaw, was the leader of the trio that tried to gun him
down in the lake-front saloon. Well, retribution had
been swift for him.

Turning out the wideloopers' pockets revealed
nothing of significance save a surprising large sum
of money, which he replaced. He regretted that their

horses had followed the others down the slope; the brands might possibly have told him something. It was unlikely, however.

Next he turned his attention to the tired cows that had scattered and were grazing. What the devil to do with them? He did not care to sit up till daybreak with them and he did not consider it advisable to leave them where they were. Just a chance that the rustlers, after they had recovered somewhat from their fright, might sneak back for them. Not apt to happen, but such gentry sometimes did the unexpected. Abruptly he arrived at a solution.

It was but a few miles farther west to Keith Norman's ranchhouse. Why not drive the herd there, where they would be safe? The brands showed they were John Fletcher's Diamond F stock. Norman would send a man to notify Fletcher and the Diamond F owner could retrieve them. Give him a chance, also, to pay Norman the visit he had promised, a bit ahead of time. With a chuckle he flipped the bit back into Shadow's mouth and tightened the cinches. Then he rolled and lighted a cigarette, giving the purloined cattle a chance to rest a bit longer and fill their bellies.

Getting the beefs moving in the right direction was no chore for a cowhand of El Halcon's ability. Soon the disgusted critters were trudging west, voicing their protest against such outlandish treatment from time to time.

Dawn was pulsing scarlet and gold in the east when he sighted the ranchhouse. Everybody was still asleep, but hammering on the front door soon brought old Keith thumping barefoot down the stairs to open it with a profane inquiry as to who was disturbing his rest.

His irritation quickly changed to a welcome greeting when he recognized his untimely guest. Slade indicated his four-footed charges, who were continuing their interrupted meal, and explained how he came to have them in tow. Old Keith proceeded to do some really fancy swearing.

"And you did for two of the sidewinders, you say?" he concluded. "Good! Good! Shut the door and sit down; I'll rustle some coffee and a snack. Pedro will be up any minute now and he'll lend a hand. I'll care for your horse. Sit down, here comes Jerry; guess she heard me call your name and had to take time to make herself beautiful before showing up."

Glancing at her tripping down the stairs in a clinging silken robe, Slade felt if that was the reason for her delay, she had succeeded admirably, even though her curly hair was touseled enough to refute her uncle's deduction.

"Why should I take time to comb it?" she replied to Slade's jocular comment. "Haven't you seen—say! What have you been into now? There's a hole in your shirt sleeve, your hat is all beat up, and there's dried blood on your forehead!"

The story was repeated, briefly, for her benefit. She shuddered, and said, "Always something nobody else would think of! I heard you knock and knew it could be nobody else showing up at this outlandish hour. Well, I'm glad you made it here so soon. I'll give Uncle Keith a hand in the kitchen."

"I'll send somebody to tell Fletcher to come and get his stock," Norman called. "Reckon he'll be sorta surprised."

"And have somebody notify the sheriff," Slade replied. "He'll want to pick up the bodies."

"Sure for certain," old Keith promised.

Without too much difficulty, Slade put away the coffee and the sumptuous snack, after which old Keith said, "And now to bed with you, pronto; you must be tuckered."

"Do feel a mite weary," Slade admitted. "Was quite a night."

In the comfortable bed he had occupied before, he slept soundly until shortly after noon. When he descended to the living room, he found Jerry awaiting him.

"Your breakfast will be ready soon," she said. "Don't talk till you've had your coffee. All men are grouchy till they've had their morning coffee."

"Yes?"

"Well, so I've been told," she giggled, and whisked out to the kitchen.

It was late afternoon when John Fletcher arrived with a couple of hands to claim his stock. He thanked Slade profusely and expressed gratification at the downing of the two rustlers.

"All you have to do is stick around for a spell and everything will be taken care of," he declared. "Sure we'll spend the night, Keith; don't feel up to night drive with those critters."

Still later, Sheriff Carter showed up, accompanied by a deputy and a couple of mules bearing the bodies of the two wideloopers, which were placed in the barn for safe keeping till the next day.

"House going to be plumb filled up tonight," Norman chuckled. "Fine! I like company, and we got plenty of room, and I expect I can rustle a bottle or two. I figure a little celebrating is in order."

"If things are too crowded, I'll sleep under a tree," Slade told Jerry, who made a face at him.

"You and your hunches!" the sheriff snorted after

receiving the details of what happened. "Well, they always seem to pay off."

"He calls them hunches, but they're really just the result of a passel of careful thinking out," commented Fletcher.

"I figure you've got something there, John," Carter conceded.

When he got an opportunity to talk with him alone, Slade informed the sheriff of his discovery that one of the wideloopers was a member of the trio that attempted to take his life in the lake-front saloon.

"So that sidewinder got what was coming to him fast," Carter exclaimed with satisfaction.

"Yes, and I consider it confirms my belief that the bunch, well organized, shrewd and capable, is working out of Amarillo, with somebody of good repute heading it," Slade said.

"I've a notion you're right," the sheriff agreed.

But he was as puzzled as El Halcon over the riddle of how cattle were run across the "waterless" desert.

"It just don't make sense," he declared. "How *do* the hellions do it?"

"I don't know," Slade admitted frankly, "but I intend to find out. I've got a couple of theories I am going to put to work. Once down in the southwest part of the state I found water on a desert where there was not supposed to be any. It was on top of what everybody considered to be a big sand dune, which in reality was a rocky hillock sheathed by wind-drifted sand over the course of ages. On top of the hillock was a wide indenture or cup that was fed by springs deep down in the earth. But I'm ready to swear there is no such formation on this desert.

"However, there evidently is water somewhere between here and the New Mexico hills. Lots of things in this great sparsely inhabited land that are supposed not to exist. I doubted it before, but now I'll be willing to put credence in the claim of oldtimers that the Indians knew where to find water out there. And if they could find it, why can't I?"

"If it's there, you'll find it," Carter predicted confidently. "Let's go in, Pedro's yelpin' to come and get it."

Dinner in the big dining room was a gala affair. After pipes and cigarettes were smoked, old Keith announced—

"Gents, now we're going to have some music. In front, everybody!"

Quickly the living room was crowded. Old Keith motioned to Jerry's grand piano.

"Ladies and—lady, rather—and gents, the singingest man in the whole dadburned Southwest will favor us with a tune or two. Go to it, Slade!"

With a smile and a nod, Slade sat down on the stool. His slender fingers drew booming chords from the really fine instrument. Then he sang, sang in a voice deep and powerful as the flooded Canadian thundering in its sunken gorge, sweetly melodious as the winds whispering through the cedars on a dreamy summer night. Songs of the horse and the lonely rangeland, and the men who loved both. Songs of the turbulent towns with their flow and rush of life, filled with their laughter, their anger, blood and death.

And as the great metallic baritone-bass pealed its magic under the low ceiling, something of it all passed through the minds of the entranced listeners, and many a thought of lonely men turned elsewhere as he concluded with a hauntingly beautiful love song of his own composition; and Jerry Norman's beautiful eyes were not the only ones that were misty.

The piano crashed its vibrating chords, and was still. Slade flashed the irresistible smile of El Halcon at his audience and left the stool. And old Keith repeated what had been said before—

"Why the devil does he ever have to shoot anybody? All he needs to do is sing to them and owlhoots turn into little harmless puppy dogs!"

"*Ai*," murmured old Pedro, the cook. "He sings as sang the Heavenly Host. But when he sings, some evil one will weep!"

Prophetic words.

Chapter Seven

As he and Carter and the deputy started for town, leading the grimly burdened mules, Fletcher following with the retrieved cows, Slade turned and gazed westward to where loomed Tucumcari, the mountains that looked like the breasts of a sleeping woman, and Mt. Capulin, the last of the active volcanoes of the southwestern United States. Somewhere on the gray desolation between the fertile rangeland and those shadowy peaks lay the answer to the tantalizing riddle that defied him. Somewhere out there was water, or all signs failed. Well, it was up to him to find it and by so doing smash the widelooping bunch that was plaguing the section. He turned back in the saddle, the concentration furrow deep between his black brows, a sure sign El Halcon was doing some hard thinking.

Did the devils confine their activities to cow stealing it wouldn't be too bad; but they undoubtedly also went in for such nice sidelines as robbery and murder.

The mystery of the hidden water was intriguing, but a much more important problem confronted him, that of learning the identity of the head of the outlaw organization, who made the plans and directed operations. Slade felt pretty sure he was somebody thoroughly familiar with the section and its possibilities. According to old Estaban, the Valley dweller, he knew of a crossing other than the one utilized the night Fletcher's cows were stolen, one that Slade himself did not know about. Also, Slade shrewdly suspected he was somebody in a position to garner information and take advantage of opportunities thus provided. Once again the new type of criminal that was invading the West, employing the methods of big city malefactors, staying in the background as much as possible and directing operations from under cover.

Slade wondered if he had been one of the wide-looping bunch whose plans he had frustrated. Somebody had certainly spoken with authority when the order to get the blankety-blank out of there was shouted. That denoted fast and accurate thinking, for unless a chance shot had downed him, holed up in the brush as he was with his targets in the brilliant flood of the moonlight, he would have killed every member of the bunch did they remain in the open and endeavor to shoot it out with him. Somebody re-alized that and reacted accordingly.

Well, he had gone up against that sort before, and so far had always come out on top. He rode on with a tranquil mind.

Progress with the laden mules was slow and the afternoon was well along when the cortege reached Amarillo. The XT hand who, the day before, brought the word to Sheriff Carter had spread the tale around and very quickly a crowd of the curious and the in-terested trailed along to the sheriff's office. The latter included several cattlemen who had recently lost stock and their satisfaction was great. One and all they shook hands with Slade and showered him with congratulations.

"Carter's been needin' a deputy like you for quite a spell, now," one oldtimer remarked. "Ain't the first time you've been in this section, is it? I recall hearing what you did to some rapscallions the last time you were here. Keep up the good work!"

Among those who visited the office was big, irascible Neale Ditmar, who had recently bought his Tumbling D spread, and of whom Sheriff Carter did not overly approve. He looked Slade up and down with his arrogant eyes, then solemnly shook hands.

"Be seeing you again," he said, and left. The sheriff's gaze followed him.

"I can't make that hellion out," he confided in an undertone to Slade. "He sorta makes a feller feel that he's laughing at you, inside. Sure don't talk much. Nobody knows for sure just where he came from. From over east is about all he's ever said."

Slade himself had not made up his mind relative to Neale Ditmar. He was something in the nature of an enigma, and enigmas always interested El Halcon, although it had been his experience that they usually turned out to be on the commonplace side. He reserved judgment on Ditmar until he learned more about him and had a chance to study him a bit.

A more congenial visitor was Tobar Shaw, the Bradded H owner to the west of Keith Norman's holding. After complimenting Slade, he chatted amicably with the sheriff.

"I just got in town and heard of Mr. Slade's exploit," he observed. "It was good hearing to me. I'll have to admit that of late I've been getting a mite worried. Big fellows like Fletcher and Norman can take it, for a while, but the little fellow, like myself, can't. Did I lose a shipping herd, I'd find myself in straitened circumstances. Even a small bunch now and then hurts."

Which Slade knew to be true. Even the big owners

could not for long withstand a steady drain on their resources. Organized widelooping had forced more than one rancher to the wall, and not always the small ones.

"A nice sort of feller," Carter remarked after Shaw had left the office. "We could use more of his sort in place of some we've been getting of late."

Slade did not argue the point pro or con, although he admitted that Tobar Shaw made a good impression. As in the case of Ditmar, he had not formed a definite opinion relative to Shaw; he was not in the habit of exercising snap judgment where anybody he met was concerned, having learned from experience that men are not always what they appear to be. Neale Ditmar might be all right despite his somewhat forbidding exterior, but then again he could be just the opposite.

The crowd had pretty well dissipated, only a few curious stragglers remaining. The sheriff shooed them out and shut the door.

"Suppose we amble over to the Trail End for a surrounding?" he said to Slade. "Nobody will admit knowing those two hellions there on the floor and there's no sense in sticking around longer right now."

Slade was agreeable and they made their way to Sanders' place, where Swivel-eye had an uproarious welcome for them.

"One out of my private bottle!" he boomed, waving said bottle in the air. "This calls for a mite of a celebration. So you hit those wind spiders where it hurt, Mr. Slade?"

"Guess two of 'em got sorta 'hurt,' and I've a notion another one ain't feeling any too good about now," the sheriff observed dryly. "A Winchester slug sorta discommodes you no matter where it nicks you. Much obliged, Swivel-eye. Yep, I can stand another one."

While they were eating, Neale Ditmar came in accompanied by three of his hands, one hobbling along with the aid of a makeshift crutch. Sheriff Carter stared at him.

"Where do you figure you hit that sidewinder the other night?" he asked Slade.

"Now don't go jumping to conclusions," the Ranger cautioned. "Lots of ways a man can hurt his leg."

"Uh-huh, *lots* of ways," grunted Carter, biting savagely on a hunk of steak.

After they finished their meal and a smoke, Slade said, "Suppose we pay Doc Beard a visit?"

"Okay by me," replied the sheriff, giving him a curious glance but asking no questions.

They found the doctor in his office cleaning some instruments. He waved them to chairs.

"What's the matter?" he asked. "Carter seein' snakes again? The last time it was centipedes with chilblains." Slade countered with a question of his own, "Treated any gunshot wounds lately, Doc?"

"Yep," Beard replied. "That's why I'm cleaning things up. Just a little while ago I worked on one of Neale Ditmar's hands. Young hellion said he was cleaning his gun and it went off; drilled a slice through his left thigh."

Sheriff Carter gave a derisive snort, and glanced significantly at Slade. El Halcon asked another question, "Did you happen to note what course the bullet took?"

"Yep," Beard repeated, "it slanted sorta down, as was to be expected." Carter shot Slade a puzzled look.

"Why the devil did you ask that?" he said.

"Because," Slade replied, "you will recall that the other night I was standing on the ground, while the man I shot was mounted on a horse. Under such circumstances, the muzzle of my rifle would be tilted up a mite and it is rather unlikely that a bullet from it would take a downward course."

"I see," nodded Carter. "So that lets the jigger out, eh?"

"Not necessarily," Slade replied. "A bullet can be deflected, say by a concha on a pair of chaps, or a holstered gun, and its course changed."

"Dadblast it!" wailed the sheriff, "you've got me all mixed up. "First you make it look like Ditmar and his bunch are in the clear, then you make it look like maybe they ain't. Come clean, now, do you suspect Ditmar?"

"Brian," Slade answered, "circumstances being what they are in this section, everybody is suspect. In a court of law, a person is adjudged innocent until proven guilty. With a Ranger trying to solve a case, the reverse obtains. I have formed no conclusion relative to Neale Ditmar or anybody else, and I can't until I have what I consider conclusive evidence of somebody's guilt. Yes, right now everybody is suspect, even you and Doc."

"I can speak for myself, but I'd rather not say about him," Doc said cheerfully, regarding the sheriff with a disapproving eye. "Oh, I reckon you can rule him out; he's too spavined and weighted down with years to pull a widelooping. Chances are he'd go to sleep and fall out of the hull."

"I'll watch a goose walk across your grave, you darned old decrepit fossil," retorted the sheriff.

Having mutually affronted each other, they had a drink from a bottle Doc produced, while Slade settled for a cup of coffee—Doc always having a pot steaming on his stove.

"Well, it 'pears we didn't learn much," Carter remarked as they headed back to the office.

"Nothing definite," Slade agreed, "but no angle should be overlooked, nor anything that might possibly provide a lead."

"That's right," said the sheriff. "So I guess we'd better open up for a while in case some more folks want to take a look at those carcasses. Just a waste of time, the chances are, but as you say, we mustn't miss any bets."

"Yes, it's just possible that somebody might recall seeing them and with whom they were associating," Slade agreed.

A few people wandered in after Carter opened the office, not many, and he was about ready to close up shop and call it a night when a man entered who Slade thought had a vaguely familiar look. He studied the bodies on the floor, then turned to El Halcón.

"Do you remember me, Mr. Slade?" he asked. "I served you a drink the other night in the Deuces Up, down by the lake."

"Yes, now I do," Slade replied.

"It was the night you had the ruckus with those three hellions who, I figure, came in with a killing in mind. Well, the big one there was one of 'em, the one you punched in the jaw."

"Yes, I recognized him," Slade admitted. "Do you know him?"

The bartender shook his head. "Nope, didn't know either of them," he said. "Well, they were in the place a while before you came in. I remembered them because somehow I didn't like their looks. Behaved themselves, all right, stood drinking and talking together and sorta watching the door. Another feller came in and had a drink with them and talked to them for a minute or so."

"Did you know him?" Slade asked abruptly, much interested.

The barkeep again shook his head. "Didn't remember ever seeing him before," he answered.

"Remember what he looked like?" the Ranger asked.

"Didn't pay much attention to him, was real busy at the time," said the drink juggler. "Just remember he was a tall feller and sort of wide in the shoulders. He was better dressed than the other three; I figured him to be a ranch owner. Didn't pay him much mind for, as I said, I was busy. He had one drink, said something or other to those fellers and went out. When I happened to look that way again, the other three were gone. A little later you came in and you know what happened next."

"Remember anything more about them?" Slade queried.

"Nothing much," the bartender said. "The boss had a swamper throw some water over them and they got their senses back—don't think they were much hurt—and then he shoved 'em out. I wouldn't have paid the whole business much mind—we ever now and then have a ruckus in the place—but as I said, I just didn't like their looks."

"And do you think you'd recognize the man who came in and talked to them, if you saw him again?"

Once more the bartender shook his head. "I doubt it," he replied. "As I said, I was sorta busy at the time and just glanced at him as I poured his drink. I might, though, if he came in and ordered a drink the same way; can't tell."

"You say he was dressed like a ranch owner?" interpolated the sheriff.

"Sorta, I'd say," the bartender agreed.

"And he was big and tall?"

"That's the way I remember him. Uh-huh, I'm sure he was a sorta tall feller. Not as tall as Mr. Slade, but not short, either."

"Hmmm!" said the sheriff. Slade smiled at the bartender.

"You may have been a big help," he said. "Thank you, very much, for coming in."

"I was just sorta curious," said the other. "We get some purty rough characters in the Deuces Up every now and then, and I was just wondering if I'd seen these fellers in there. Well, got to get on the job. Be seeing you."

"What do you think?" the sheriff asked Slade after the drink juggler had departed.

"I don't know," the Ranger admitted frankly. "There are a number of ranch owners in the section, and some of them are tall. Quite a few would answer to that vague description."

"I can think of one it fits sorta well," the sheriff remarked pointedly.

"Yes, but no positive identification, so take it easy," Slade advised. The sheriff subsided to mutterings.

"Well, guess that was all," he said, glancing around the empty room. "Suppose we amble over to the Trail End and then call it a day. I'm feeling a mite tuckered."

Chapter Eight

Again it was Slade's amazingly keen hearing that saved them. It was but the faintest whisper of metallic sound, a key turning slowly in the lock of the back door, but it was a thunderclap warning to El Halcon's ears. His arm shot out and hurled Sheriff, chair, and lamp to the floor. Black darkness fell like a thrown blanket even as Slade went half way across the room in a sideways leap, both guns blazing as the back door banged open. Answering shots flamed the darkness. Slugs whizzed past, thudded into the wall. One grazed the back of his left hand.

Then he heard a queer gurgling cry followed by the thud of something falling. He fired twice at the sound, shifting position as he pulled trigger. There were no answering reports. He hesitated a moment, straining his ears, then glided forward, guns ready for action. Outside was a clatter of hoofs, fading into the distance.

The sheriff was roaring profanity and surging to his feet. "Get a light going," Slade called to him, his gaze riveted on a shadowy shape lying just inside the door. Carter started to obey, fell over the smashed chair and swore weirdly. Again he scrambled to his feet and a moment later a second lamp flared, its glow falling on a dead man on the floor, blood still pulsing from his bullet-slashed throat.

Slade reloaded his guns before addressing the raving sheriff. "Guess we'd better send word to the bartender," he said, peering at the corpse's contorted face. "This is another of the three who braced me in the Deuces Up."

"You sure?" demanded Carter.

"Yes, I'm sure," Slade replied.

"Well, that's just fine!" said the sheriff. "Now if you can just get a chance to line sights with the other sidewinder! How in blazes did you catch on so fast?"

"Heard the key turning in the lock," Slade explained. "Where'd they get a key? No trouble to make one for these old locks, perhaps from a wax impression, if you know how, and evidently they know how." He dragged the body to where the others lay, placed it beside them, removed the key from the outside of the door and closed and locked it.

"Can hold an inquest over him tomorrow with the other two," he said. "Let's see what's in his pockets."

"Just another pretty good haul for the county treasury," he observed a little later. Nothing else of significance." Turning the pockets inside out, he carefully examined the seams.

"Thought so," he said. "This hellion has been out on the desert—alkali dust in the pocket seams. One of the widelooping bunch, all right, and added confirmation that they do run the cows across the desert."

"Is there anything you don't notice!" marveled the sheriff.

"Plenty," Slade answered, "but this was fairly obvious."

"Dadblast it, looks like no place is safe anymore!" snorted Carter.

"And it might be a good notion for you to sort of avoid my company," Slade said. "I don't think they are after you personally, but as you told Jerry Norman, flying lead plays no favorites."

"Like the blankety-blank so-and-so I will!" the sheriff bawled indignantly. "Only next time give me a chance to get in on the fun, instead of hoggin' it all yourself."

"Didn't have time to notify you," Slade replied cheerfully. "Figured you were better on the floor with the light out."

"Like to busted my neck over that blankety-blank chair," Carter growled, giving the remains a kick.

Voices sounded outside, then a tentative knock on the front door. Standing to one side, Slade opened to admit two men, both of whom the sheriff called by name.

"Did you hear it, Sheriff?" asked the one addressed as Bruff. "We thought we heard shootin' over this way."

"Guess you did," replied Carter, "A gent ambled in the back door without an invite and caught himself a dose of lead pizening."

The two men stared. "You mean he tried to gun the sheriff's office?" he asked incredulously.

"Sure 'peared that way," said Carter. "Anyhow him and one or two more sure burned a heap of powder. Look at the wall over there, and there's blood on Slade's hand. Take a look at that devil, maybe you've seen him before."

The pair studied the body, then shook their heads. "Never saw him before, or the other two hellions either," said Bruff.

"Now I *am* going to call it a night," declared the sheriff. "And I need two snorts, not just one. Outside! Outside! And let's head for the Trail End."

When they reached the saloon, Slade and the

sheriff occupied a table, the latter ordering a double snort, Slade a sandwich and a cup of coffee. Bruff and his companion hustled to the bar and began talking excitedly to associates there. Soon the table was surrounded by the curious demanding details. The sheriff supplied them.

High indignation was expressed over the attempt at snake-blooded murder, and Slade warmly praised for frustrating it.

"And I wouldn't be a bit surprised if one of those blabbermouths was the hellion who ordered it done," Carter observed cynically when they were alone. "Blast it! I'm looking sideways at everybody!"

"We are sort of in the same corral," Slade replied, with a smile. "I don't know which way to look; appears I'm getting exactly nowhere."

"Oh, you're doing all right," Carter said. "You're thinning 'em out, and that helps. Just a matter of time till you have the whole nest of scorpions on the run."

Slade hoped the sheriff was right, but personally he was not inclined to view the matter in so thoroughly an optimistic light; he felt that he had made but little real progress. His plan to bring the outlaws to him had worked out, to an extent, but so far he had only been able to knock off a few rather incompetent hired hands. The main problem still confronted him, for he had not the slightest idea of who was the brains of the outfit; the hellion was keeping well in the background. And until his identity was definitely established and he was eliminated, the problem remained unsolved.

Getting John Fletcher and Clyde Brent together was something, and so was the frustrating of the widelooping try, but only incidental to his paramount objective. Well, maybe he'd get a break, they usually seemed to come, sooner or later, and he was firmly convinced that right would triumph in the end. He went to bed and slept soundly.

The inquest on the three dead outlaws was held the following afternoon, Doc Beard, the coroner, presiding. The jury's verdict was laconic and typically cow country. Slade was complimented on doing a good chore but advised not to let any of the varmints escape, next time. Sheriff Carter bought the Court and the jury a drink.

"Now what?" asked Carter, glancing expectantly at the Ranger.

"Now," Slade replied, "I'm going to wander about town a bit and see if I can learn anything. Somebody might drop a word that would be significant."

"Or do something significant," Carter grunted. "Watch your step."

Promising to do so, Slade began his amble. He visited place after place of various sorts, listened to scraps of conversation, studied faces, talked with acquaintances and learned—nothing. Finally he leaned against a convenient post, rolled a cigarette and stood gazing across the sheet of water now known as Amarillo Lake.

Amarillo, then called Ragtown, had its beginning in a collection of buffalo-hide huts that were occupied by buffalo hunters, bone pickers, and railroad builders. Lumber was costly and had to be brought from a distance. Buffalo-hides were plentiful, convenient, and cheap. Even the hotel had walls, partitions, and a roof made of buffalo-hides. They were somewhat odoriferous and as they aged, they became quite transparent, so that lights inside revealed some startling secrets; there was little privacy in Ragtown, which did not particularly bother the rambunctious inhabitants. Only the saloons were decently domiciled of lumber freighted from a distance.

Then a well-heeled and ambitious gentleman by the name of Sanborn had an idea and proceeded to put it into effect. He had faith in the settlement's future and exercised that faith by laying out a town site southeast of Ragtown, at a point where the railroad tracks curved around the body of water then known as Wild Horse Lake. Apparently with a poetic leaning, Mr. Sanborn named his town Oneida, an Indian dialect word meaning star. However, it would seem the stars were not favorable to Mr. Sanborn's project. The rains came, the lake scrambled over its banks, and Mr. Sanborn found his stock yards, railroad station, and other buildings placidly standing in four feet of water.

Mr. Sanborn said things that were not nice and moved his town away from there, farther from the blankety-blank lake. It was rumored that he first contemplated renaming his settlement Jinx Town, but somebody happened to mention the yellow amaryllis flowers that blanket the prairie with gold in the springtime. Mr. Sanborn, still poetic, was intrigued and renamed his town Amarillo.

It would appear the flowers were more friendly than the stars and the new town prospered. Out of gratitude to the flowery cups of gold, Mr. Sanborn painted his buildings a bright yellow.

Mr. Sanborn's faith in his town was soon justified. Amarillo was a going concern, and going stronger all the time.

Surveying the terrain, Walt Slade concluded that while Mr. Sanborn was without doubt an excellent promoter, planner, and builder, he was no great shakes as a geologist. Even a rudimentary knowledge of that science would have told him that where he first laid out his town, the lake had been before and would assuredly pay a return visit. Perhaps some oldtimers like Colonel Goodnight might have forewarned him, but the oldtimers did not particularly favor the erection of the town, so they held their peace. Let Mr. Sanborn learn the hard way.

Slade was slightly inclined to envy Mr. Sanborn, who had successfully solved his problem, for the moment at least, and, so to speak, was riding the crest of the wave. Oh, well, what one could do, so could another. He was humming gaily under his breath as he headed for the Trail End and something to eat.

However, he was in a more serious mood when, several hours later—slightly after full dark, to be exact, he got the rig on Shadow and rode west by north.

Well out of Amarillo, he drew rein and for some time studied the back trail. Satisfied that he was not being followed, he rode on. Nearing the Canadian Valley, he turned due west and rode steadily hour after hour. He crossed Keith Norman's XT range and knew he was on Tobar Shaw's holding, the Bradded H.

The old Hartsook spread was long from north to south but narrow east to west, reaching to the edge of the desert and the New Mexico Territorial Line.

With the dying moon drifting westward he sighted the desert in the distance, glittering in the silvery glow. He continued until he reached a straggle of brush near the desert's edge. Here he turned south until he came to a little stream that flowed from the rangeland to soon lose itself in the thirsty sands. Drawing rein, he got the rig off Shadow and turned the big black loose to graze. Then he rolled up in his blanket and with his saddle for a pillow was soon fast asleep.

With the first tremulous rose in the east that heralded the dawn he was awake. Over a small fire of dry wood he cooked his breakfast—fried eggs and bacon and a bucket of coffee, which, with a bunch of bread, made a satisfying meal for a hungry man. Shadow did very well with a helpin' of oats from a saddle pouch.

After smoking a cigarette, Slade boiled another bucket of coffee, with which he filled a canteen. Two more canteens were filled with water for Shadow.

"Now we're all set to take a chance on that burned-over section of hell," he told the horse. "Unless my memory fails me, and I don't think it does, there are a couple more small creeks within the next few miles to the south, both flowing into the desert and sinking into the sands. That water must go somewhere and unless it penetrates deep into the earth, which I consider improbable in this geological terrain, it very likely reaches the surface again, although probably in a manner not easy to find. Well, our first chore is over here on this side of the desert, so let's go, horse, and keep your eyes peeled."

Mounting, he rode very slowly along the straggle of brush that edged the desert, surveying every inch of the ground with the greatest care. What he sought was very apt to be pretty well hidden from the casual observer, but he was confident that he would find it. If he didn't, his whole theory fell to the ground and he'd have to try and figure something else.

With the sun mounting higher, he rode on, passing one small creek, then another. He had covered a few miles but knew he was still on Tobar Shaw's Bradded H range when he found it, neatly concealed but discernible to sharp eyes that knew what to look for, like those of the Indians for whose guidance it was placed.

Chapter Nine

Upright in the ground amid the brush was the bleached shoulder bone of a huge buffalo. The enormous fan-shaped bone was about eighteen inches long and nearly a foot wide at the larger end. On the smooth white surface pictures were daubed in red, yellow and green mineral paint. They showed an Indian wigwam or *tepi*, beside which stood several Indians, the small pictures surprisingly accurate as to detail. One appeared to be cooking over a fire. Another was drinking from a horn cup. Two more were approaching the camp from the east, and scattered about were several head of cattle.

To Walt Slade the message was as clear as it had been to those who were guided by it many years before. Where the camp was made, far out on the desert, there was water. Just where, the message did not show—which was to be expected. But to those who, unfamiliar with the area, came later, it was "writing" as plain as any utilized by white men. As plain as the ancient Egyptians' hieroglyphics, who also employed pictures to convey their thoughts to others.

For a long time, Slade studied the pictures, hoping to hit on some clue that would indicate the exact location of the water, but failed to do so. The best he could hope for was the general direction in which it lay. He had a very good idea how to determine that.

Squatting down, he sighted carefully over the top of the blade, raised his eyes to the shadowy hills far,

far to the west, back to the bone again, and got his bearings, the course he should follow, in relation to certain landmarks supplied by the hill formation. Straightening up, he gazed westward over the pitiless waste of sand and alkali now shimmering with heat. He knew well what that desolation could do, bewildering the brain and choking the throat, deceiving the hapless wanderer with mirages of rippling streams and lakes where none existed until he succumbed to gabbling delirium and death. That was the desert, and did he not find water somewhere near the middle of it, he might well never live to reach those distant hills.

However, his horse was strong, well fed and rested, and Slade was not unfamiliar with the dangers and hardships of a desert. Would be safer to wait until the comparative cool of night, but that would greatly lessen his chances of hitting on the hidden water which was his goal. He decided to risk it. If he had misread the implied direction of the desert signboard, the blade bone, he could perish miserably, for there was nothing else to guide him. The desert was trackless. Always as the dark closed down, a wind would rise, shifting the sands, quickly erasing any hoofprints of horses or cattle passing across its surface. But he believed the bone dependable. Anyhow, he'd gamble on it being so.

The desert was white, with the awful whiteness of dessication and death, glaring under the sun, flinging forth its warning and its threat, as desolate and uninviting a region as El Halcon had ever viewed, as solemn and quiet and as alien to man as the star-studded midnight sky, grim, relentless, waiting.

And yet, it was not without a beauty all its own— the terrible beauty of the wastelands with their utter silence and their utter peace, ageless, everlasting, cradled in the lap of eternity, setting at naught the futile strivings and the petty ambitions of mankind. Slade sensed this as he mounted and sent Shadow forward.

Soon he was out on the true desert and almost instantly the heat seemed to double, triple, quadruple. It poured down from the blazing sun overhead, beat upward from the burning sands beneath, like unto the breath of a furnace. Slade felt as if it were sucking the very blood out of his veins.

However, one can get used to most anything, in a degree, and after that first devil's blast, the effect was modified. He narrowed his eyes to the glare, rendered dazzling by the hot air that danced over the surface of the desert as over a red-hot stove, breathed slowly and deeply and relaxed. And after a disgusted snort or two, Shadow appeared to make out very well.

The desert was not totally flat. Here and there were low sand dunes. Nor was it utterly devoid of vegetation. Occasional straggles of mesquite broke the white monotony, its tremendous root system evidently able to suck up enough moisture in time of rain to allow it to exist. And as he forged on and on, he encountered infrequent dry washes, through which water must have flowed during heavy downpours. These interested him, for they appeared to substantiate, slightly, the theory he had formed as to the existence, if it did exist, of the hidden water to which the Indian signboard pointed.

From time to time he took a sip of his coffee, now heated to about the temperature of a man's blood. Each time he dismounted and poured water into his cupped hands for Shadow, enough for a couple of swallows. Shadow sucked up the fluid greedily and asked for more, but his rider vetoed the request.

"May have to make last what we've got to the other side of this scorched griddle, or back the way we came, whichever seems advisable," he warned. "Besides, too much can make you sick, as you know well as I do."

Shadow snorted general disagreement to the jobation which did not seem to impress him much, but let it go at that.

The sun crossed the zenith and slid down the western sky, and El Halcon began to grow anxious. He reckoned he was just about midway the desert, and he didn't like the look of the southwestern sky, which hinted at wind, and wind raising the sand and alkali in blinding clouds could be deadly. The hills seemed no nearer than when he started out in their direction.

"We should hit it soon, if we're going to hit it at all," he muttered. "This is getting a mite serious."

It was, for the blazing heat and the eternal glare were beginning to have their effect. His tongue was swelling, his eyes seemed filmed, and there was a singing in his ears—warning signs that heat prostration or sunstroke might well be in the offing, and not too far off, either.

Then he saw something that quickened his pulses and cleared his befogged mind. Directly ahead and no great distance away was a long and wide dry wash along the edges of which grew a more abundant than average stand of mesquite. And without apparent reason, Shadow quickened his pace a little.

"Do you smell it, feller?" Slade asked. "If you do, it's more than I can."

The sides of the wash, which was much narrower

at the bottom than at the top, sloped downward at a fairly steep angle, but he discovered a place where sure-footed Shadow could negotiate the descent.

Once at the bottom of the wash, things improved a bit, for there were places where the rushing water of flood times had hollowed out the lower banks until wide overhangs provided a grateful shade.

Under one he dismounted, loosened the cinches a bit and gave the horse a little more of the precious water. Then he sat down with his back against the bank and rolled and smoked a cigarette, after a couple of sips from his coffee canteen.

He smoked slowly, resting, relaxing until his pulses were back to normal and his eyes had cleared. Pinching out the butt and casting it aside, he examined the bottom of the wash. It was of hard-packed sand, much firmer than that of the surrounding desert, a phenomenon the discovery of which filled him with satisfaction.

"Horse," he said, "I believe it's going to work out. I once before encountered something similar. Yes, I believe we'll hit it. Let's see, now."

Moving to the edge of the slope he studied the ground with great care. His feeling of satisfaction increased when he found, hugging the ground, a film of green, a scattering of tiny plants of the algae family, related to pond scum, plants that could not exist without moisture—which meant the existence of water they could tap.

But where was the water? Nowhere was there a drop in sight, only the endless, weird expanse of sand and alkali. Slade straightened up, walked to where Shadow stood looking expectant, tightened the cinches and mounted.

"Now, feller, it's up to you," he said. "A bunch of

cows could do it faster and easier, but I believe you can handle the chore."

Moving out onto the bottom of the wash, he headed the horse down it for a little distance, turned him and made a return trip. Shadow stepped out briskly, almost eagerly, it seemed, apparently knowing just what was expected of him and how to do it.

Back and forth he plodded, back and forth, back and forth. Slowly the hard-packed sand began to sink under the steady beat of his hoofs, until he was moving in a narrow shallow trench. The pitiless sun poured down its burning rays. They flashed back from the sands. But Shadow never hesitated, back and forth, back and forth. Now the hard-packed sand was growing a trifle mushy. A few more minutes and little sparkles were oozing up into the trench, back and forth, back and forth. Now the gallant horse was pounding his hoofs through a film of what was undoubtedly water, back and forth, back and forth! Now the water was over his hoofs. Once released, it surged upward swiftly until it was ankle deep. A little more and Slade called a halt. The trench was filled to the brim with clear, sparkling, and cool water.

"Help yourself," he invited.

Shadow plunged his nose in and drank and drank. Slade dismounted and had a long swig himself. Then, while Shadow desisted for a spell, before drinking some more, he filled the water canteens to the brim, drank the last of his coffee and replaced it with water. Stoppering the canteens, he tucked them into the saddle pouches.

"Come, feller," he said. Shadow followed him to the shade of the overhang. Slade emptied the remainder of the oats onto the ground, drew a couple of slices of bread with bacon between them, and man and horse enjoyed a satisfying meal.

"Where did the water come from?" El Halcon replied to a hypothetical question from Shadow. "Geologically speaking the explanation is quite simple. Down there under the sand is a cup-shaped ledge of rock, something in the nature of a trough, scoured out by the action of water untold ages ago, for all this section was once a great inland sea or lake. Rain water seeps through the sand into the rock trough. Of course it cannot permeate the stone, but it does hold up the hard-packed sand, the bottom of the layer being also impervious to water. Perhaps also there is water seepage from those small creeks we encountered over on the rangeland. There the water remains. Under the pounding of your hoofs, a portion of the sand layer sinks, the water filters through and reaches the surface. Before long it will sink again and no trace of it will be left. Long ago the Indians discovered it and figured how to obtain it. Somebody else also understands the geological formation and its possibilities. Who? That I don't know, yet, and I wish I did. But it is a simple explanation of how a bunch of cows can be run across the desert to the New Mexico hills and market. The cattle are allowed to rest here under the overhang—I've already noticed very faint traces of hoof marks the wind-driven sand of evening hasn't totally obliterated, under that further overhang, which is more shallow than this one. Didn't pay much attention to them, didn't even mention them to you, for I knew just what to look for already. Get the idea?"

Shadow snorted his understanding and nosed up the few remaining oats.

"Well, we found it, but I'm hanged if I know what to do with it," his master added. "We could intercept a stolen herd here, but I'm not at all sure it would do much good. We've got to learn who is the head of the outfit, somebody who was either able to piece together old Indian legends or has the geological knowledge necessary to understand this unusual but by no means isolated phenomenon. Somebody who perhaps has in mind something more outstanding than widelooping and robbery which may but be the means to an end."

Slowly the water sank back out of sight, and as it sank, the liquified sands rose. The wind-drift would finish the chore and soon there would be left no sign of Shadow's industrious plodding. Slade watched the water vanish and remarked reflectively—

"There is a vast subterranean watershed beneath all this section. Some day folks will realize its potentialities and take advantage of them. Artesian wells will replace the primitive windmill and Amarillo and other towns will be relieved of water shortage. Okay, horse, I guess we'd better be moving in some direction."

For a few minutes he debated the advisability of staying in the shade of the overhang until after nightfall. It would be far the wiser course, but he was anxious to get back to Amarillo as quickly as possible, even after studying the ominous southwest.

Down there were higher dunes, misty with distance, and from their crests flung forth long and broad streamers that glinted in the sun, like to the banners of an advancing army. That, Slade knew, meant wind, and getting caught in a wind storm out on the desert was nothing to joke about. However, he decided to risk it. Giving Shadow another drink, and taking a couple of swallows himself, he mounted and turned east through the blaze of the sunshine, the sands whispering under his mount's hoofs, the only sound to break the deathly silence of the wastelands.

"Yes," he concluded for Shadow's benefit, who didn't appear particularly interested, "some day there will be garden spots where now is only desolation, the desert lands will blossom and folks yet unborn will find prosperity and happiness. Worth working for, horse. Let's go, the sun's crawling west and it'll be a bit cooler after a while, I hope."

Chapter Ten

Shadow stepped out briskly, despite the heat, knowing very well he was homeward bound to his comfortable stall and oats. His rider kept casting anxious glances toward the southwest. Now the far distant sand hills had vanished and there the desert was a strange purplish-blue, an unearthly and sinister shade. The wind was strengthening and lifting the sands to form a smoky veil shot with lurid flickers like to lightning behind a cloud. Slade began to regret that he had left the comparative safety of the sheltering overhang in the dry wash. Looked very much like they were going to be caught by a desert storm. The heat seemed to be, if anything, increasing and the air had a creamy feel that made breathing a labored effort.

On and on forged the tall black horse, pitting his superb strength and endurance against the grim, imponderable forces of nature at its worst. From time to time, Slade halted to give him a little water and a chance to catch his breath, then on and on toward where the hospitable rangeland lay somewhere beyond the ever retreating horizon.

Everything considered, they were making good time, but that threatening dust cloud in the southwest was traveling just a little faster. Slade figured they had covered perhaps two-thirds the distance they had to go and the sun was low in the west when the storm struck.

Instantly the heat increased. The air was filled with flying yellow shadows, the wind-driven sand beat against horse and rider like a living thing of utter malevolence. Unsuspected flecks of gravel were raised from the desert floor to sting the flesh like spent bullets. One minute the sky was utterly shrouded, then the sun was visible, a weird magenta color, like to the full moon seen through haze, to vanish again as the dust cloud thickened and the eerie yellow shadows swooped down.

Leaning forward in the saddle, his hatbrim drawn low, his neckerchief over his nose and mouth, Slade endured the torment as best he could. He knew his horse's struggle was exhausting, but there was nothing to do but keep going and hope to outdistance the storm. To halt would be fatal.

His mind began to cloud, crawling with spectral elements that gnawed at his brain like illusive maggots, vanished but to return again to their ghostly attack. Then gradually their torture was replaced by a deep and drowsy happiness that stole over him on treacherous little cat-feet. The forerunner to the dark borderland of desert madness that would quickly deliver him to death. Barely in time he sensed his deadly danger. He flung back his head, slapped his cheeks with one hand after the other, hard, stinging blows that jolted him back to normalcy. He straightened in the saddle, grimly faced the beat of the wind; he'd whip the damned thing yet.

But now Shadow was blowing hard, lurching, his steady gait changed to a weaving shamble; did he fall, he would never rise again.

Slade swung down from the saddle, looped the reins over his arm and talked soothingly to the exhausted horse, who, relieved of his weight, picked up a bit. And responsibility revived El Halcon's strength, to a degree. Shadow had done his part. Now it was up to him to save the faithful animal from destruction. He slogged doggedly ahead, stumbling, reeling, each step an agonizing effort. His chest labored and he coughed retchingly. Half delirious, he cursed the wind, the sand, and the heat.

"Damn you, I'll beat you yet!" he croaked from his scorched throat. Over and over he said it, until the words were like a rumbling drum in his ears. "I'll beat you yet! I'll beat you yet!" He felt there was nothing to him except the will that thundered to him—"*Hold on!*"

He did. And his indomitable courage was rewarded. Abruptly the air cleared. The wind still howled, but now it was a clean blast, invigorating, revivifying. Numbly he realized that instead of crunching sand there was whispering grass beneath his feet. His bleary eyes were smitten by the rays of the setting sun, rosy, friendly rays like to the love-light in a woman's eyes. Slowly he sank to the soft carpet of the rangeland grass and lapsed into the coma of utter exhaustion, his last words a triumphant mumble—"*I—beat—you!*"

Beside him, Shadow stood with hanging head and front legs spread wide. He gave a weak snort that seemed to echo his master's words.

Yes, they beat it, but as he gradually regained complete consciousness, Slade realized it had been as close a call for both of them as they'd ever experienced. A few more hundred yards to go and they *wouldn't* have beat it. He glanced toward the desert with a heightened respect for its devilishness.

The wind still blew, but its exultant howl had

changed to a disappointed whine, and shortly it ceased altogether.

Shadow had straightened up and looked to be about his normal self again. Slade gave him what was left of the water, mounted and rode north by east. He was outrageously thirsty and his throat felt like an overheated dry kiln, but he could hold out until they reached one of the creeks, which he knew to be not far off.

Soon he spotted its wavering silver flash and a little later he flopped from the saddle and drank his fill, first flipping the bit from Shadow's mouth so the cayuse could quench his thirst in comfort. Then, feeling greatly refreshed, he managed to roll a cigarette with fingers that still trembled a little and drew in deep and satisfying drafts of the fragrant smoke.

The sun had set and the far distant hills were crowned with crimson and the desert was a flame of color. Slade viewed its unearthly beauty with the tolerant and appreciative eye of a conqueror, a feeling quite different from that which he had entertained for it a short time before.

"And now, feller, we'll head for Keith Norman's XT ranchhouse," he told Shadow. "I'm as empty as a gutted sparrow and I've got a notion you are, too. It isn't so very far off and we're neither in any shape to make it to town tonight."

Mounting, he rode east, veering more and more to the north, and reached Norman's hospitable casa long after dark.

Old Keith opened to his knock, whooped a welcome, and bawled for a wrangler to care for Shadow.

"Say! you've sure picked up your share of dust, and you look sorta beat," he exclaimed.

"I am," Slade admitted, slumping into a chair. "Was prowling around on the desert and got caught in a wind storm," he explained, making no mention of his discovery of the hidden water, which he preferred to keep to himself for the time being.

"That desert's no place for anybody when there's a storm up; you shouldn't have took a chance with it," Norman said reprovingly. "Here comes Jerry, she'll fix you coffee and something to eat. Pedro's gone to bed; he'd be glad to get up for you, but there's no sense to it. Rustle your hocks, chick, can't you see the man's starving?"

Jerry proceeded to do so and Slade did full justice to the repast she set before him. Old Keith chuckled.

"Got more sense than most women," he declared. "Know better than to talk to a man and ask questions when he's hungry. Okay, honey, now you can turn your wolf loose on him—his belly's lined."

Later, when they were alone in the living room, Slade told her everything, because she knew what he was and why he was in the section, and he got a sound scolding for risking the desert with a storm imminent.

"You should have stayed right where you were, safe in the dry wash, until the storm had passed," she declared. "Why do you always have to take needless chances? Why all the hurry to get back?"

"Look in the mirror and you'll see why," he grinned.

"Huh!" she sniffed. "I'll wager you never thought of me once."

"I did, too," he said. "Toward the last, when I was getting a bit woozy, I saw all sorts of things including angels, and they all had your face."

"Yes, but we are taught that there are angels *and*

angels," she retorted. "I wonder just which variety you saw."

Slade chuckled and let it go at that.

"We had a visitor this afternoon," she remarked. "Mr. Neale Ditmar from over east."

"Yes?"

"Uh-huh, he said he'd heard that Uncle Keith contemplated selling out and moving elsewhere, and if so, he would very much like to have first bid on the property, that he desired to expand his holding and there was no chance to do so eastward, with John Fletcher owning the land to the east. He said Fletcher evinced no intention of moving, and that besides we would not be able to buy such a big holding."

"Yes," Slade prompted, looking interested.

"The fact is," she continued, "that right after we'd lost that last bunch of cows, Uncle Keith got mad and did say to Fletcher that he was of half a notion to sell out. Guess Fletcher passed the remark along and Ditmar heard of it. Yes," she added with a smile and a dimple, "Uncle Keith said he had *half* a notion to sell and move."

Slade chuckled, for he knew what quite likely Mr. Ditmar did not know, that Miss Geraldine Norman was half owner of the XT spread and old Keith could not sell without her consent.

"What do you think, dear, should we sell?" she asked.

"It is merely a matter of what you desire to do or desire not to do," he replied. "If you really wish to move and are offered a fair price, go ahead. But it is a good holding and will increase in value as more and more people come into the section. In my opinion, it will never be worth a fortune, but it will always make you a good living. Later, as more farmers arrive, you might very well sell them a stretch of land at a nice profit, land which they will irrigate. Agriculture is coming to the Panhandle and it will increase land values. That's the way the situation stands as I see it."

"We won't sell," Jerry replied decisively. "Among other things, now you always know where to find me instead of having to prowl all over Texas looking for me after you've run out of stops. We won't sell."

"I consider it a wise decision," he said smilingly, "and I appreciate your thoughtfulness of my convenience. Come here!"

Some time later, "And you discovered the hidden water that nobody believed existed. I think it was just about the cleverest thing I ever heard tell of."

"Not cleverness, just knowledge and experience," he deprecated. "As I said, I once before encountered something similar. Really, it was just a case of knowing what to look for."

"But something which nobody else even thought of," she said.

"Nobody is hardly the right word," he differed. "Somebody else discovered it before I did, somebody who evidently had faith in the old Indian legends and was familiar enough with their customs to also know what to look for, and with the knowledge of how it could be put to use. In this case, a reprehensible use."

"But what you learned will enable you to put a stop to the widelooping, will it not?"

"Yes, it will do that, this particular phase of it at least," he admitted. "But it far from solves the problem of who is back of what has been happening, things much more serious than cow stealing. But it is something and may provide needed opportunity."

She sighed. "But as Sheriff Carter says, you'll

eventually come out on top, of that there is no doubt in my mind. Only I'm liable to suffer a stroke or nervous prostration before you do. Oh, well, meanwhile it's nice to have you, for the time being at least. I'm glad you were able to make one of your stops here."

"Stops!"

"Uh-huh, that's the right word this time. I don't fool myself, my dear. As I think I said once before, you are irresistible to women, but the corollary, the male weakness, women are irresistible to you. 'Gather ye rosebuds while ye may!' "

She glanced at the clock.

Chapter Eleven

As he headed for town, shortly before noon the next day, Slade remarked to Shadow, "I wonder if that Ditmar gent knows something, or thinks he does? Admitting the assumption that he does know, or has been told something, he is a living example of Pope's couplet, 'A little learning is a dangerous thing.' Still assuming that he knows something, he is right so far as the over-all picture is concerned, but erroneous as to details and may be making a colossal blunder.

"All of which, of course, is pure conjecture on my part. There is no proof that the reason he gave Keith Norman for desiring to acquire his holding was not an honest reason. He could be just farsighted and realize that land values in this section will undoubtedly be on the increase before long. Well, at least he is something to think on, which so far we have sorely lacked."

Largely as a matter of habit, Slade rode watchfully, for he did not really anticipate any trouble. He kept well away from the brush fringe of the Canadian Valley and on the open prairie he had little to fear. His belief was justified, for he reached Amarillo without untoward incident.

An astounded man was Sheriff Carter as he listened to El Halcon's account of his experience on the desert.

"So it's really there," he marveled. "Water on that burned-over section of raised hell. Well, guess the oldtimers knew what they were talking about when they insisted the Injuns made that crossing with cows. I always believed it just talk, bunkhouse jabber, but I guess I was wrong."

"Folks said the same thing about the Lost Lakes Captain Arrington discovered in the desert farther south," Slade pointed out. "When definite knowledge is lost, people are wont to scoff at something that is maintained without corroborating evidence. Don't forget, geographers drew their maps with a blank place they labeled the Great American Desert—which was really the Texas Panhandle, and very far from being a desert. Even as late as 1849, Captain Marcy, a noted explorer, said, 'This country is and must remain uninhabited forever.' Well, we have before our eyes a refutation of Marcy's statement. The time is coming, and not too far off, when Amarillo's grain elevators will handle millions of bushels of wheat each season, to say nothing of barley, oats, and rye. And there will be other things that right now very few people are giving thought to. Instead of roads being marked by furrows plowed in the prairie sod, as many of them are now, there will be broad highways following the course of the old trails. Just a matter of time."

Sheriff Carter regarded him curiously. "You have faith in the Panhandle country, don't you, Walt," he stated rather than asked.

"Yes, I have faith in the Panhandle country, and in Texas, and in America," Slade replied gravely. "This is the land of opportunity. All that is needed is for each and every one of us to do his share toward making opportunity a reality."

"And you're doing your share," said the old sheriff. "You're doing your share. . . . But getting back to that blasted water you discovered, what are we going to do about it?"

"Frankly I don't know, yet," Slade admitted. "Knowing the route they take, we could very likely intercept and retrieve a stolen herd at the edge of the desert, but just how much real good it would do I'm not prepared to say. Incidentally, the southern edge of Keith Norman's range will be patrolled every night from now on—Jerry's taking care of that—and I don't think anything will get past his boys, which should help. By the way, who has been the hardest hit by the wideloopers?"

"John Fletcher and his Diamond F, far and away," the sheriff replied without hesitation. "As you know, plenty of other outfits have reported losses, but Fletcher has been catching it hot and heavy."

"I see," Slade said, his eyes thoughtful. Carter looked expectant, but the Ranger did not see fit to elaborate his remark, at the moment.

"Well, I guess a bite to eat is in order," he said. "Been quite a while since breakfast, and although it was a good one, I'm beginning to feel lank again."

"Let's go," agreed Carter. "Trail End?"

"Good as any," Slade replied.

As they sat down at a table and gave their order, Slade observed, "Fletcher is particularly vulnerable because so much of his holding is north of the Canadian Valley; but if Ditmar and Shaw could be persuaded to patrol effectively to the south, as Norman will be doing, the pressure on him would be relieved."

"Ditmar!" snorted the sheriff. "I expect Shaw will be glad to cooperate, but as to Ditmar, I ain't at all sure about that hellion, in more ways than one."

Slade nodded without comment; he was not altogether sure about *Senor* Ditmar himself.

"The owners' chief weakness," he added, "is that they have concentrated on the Canadian Valley, being convinced that the cows were run by that route to the New Mexico hills. In fact, I rather leaned to that assumption myself, at first. That bunch being run across the Valley and onto the prairie to the south changed my opinion. That was what really started me looking for hidden water in the desert."

"Well, you found it, and I've a notion it's going to just about put an end to the real widelooping hereabouts," predicted Carter.

"Perhaps," Slade conceded, "but it won't put an end to our troubles. With that source of revenue dried up, the outlaws will turn to other things. As you told me in the beginning, they have already branched out quite a bit."

"You're darned right," growled Carter. "Robbery, burglary, and murder as a sideline."

"Yes, that's the worst angle," Slade said. "A chore of rustling is usually pulled off without a killing. Incidentally, Fletcher made the mistake of guarding the southwest edge of his holding, being convinced that the wideloopers used the Canadian River route, whereas instead they struck straight across the Valley, and at more than one point, according to what old Estaban told me—which makes the task of intercepting them more difficult."

"How about the hidden water?" Carter asked. "You going to tell folks what you found?" Slade shook his head.

"Not just yet. Somebody would be sure to talk, and perhaps with the wrong pair of ears listening, which would be to our disadvantage. I may be making a mistake by not spreading the word around, but I don't believe I am. So long as the outlaws use that route across the desert, we may have a better opportunity to drop a loop on them."

"I've a notion you're right," agreed the sheriff. "What's our next move?"

"To try and anticipate what the devils have in mind," Slade replied. "Which is likely to be something of a chore."

"Uh-huh, a helluva chore," grunted Carter. "Hello! here comes Fletcher and Ditmar." He waved an invitation to the ranchers and they made their way to the table; Fletcher ordered drinks all around.

"Well, Mr. Slade, what you got to tell us now?" he asked.

"If you don't feel I am presuming, I am going to offer you a little advice," the Ranger replied.

"Shoot!" said Fletcher. "What is it? Any advice you hand out I figure worth listening to." Ditmar nodded agreement.

"Just this," Slade answered. "I understand you have been concentrating on keeping watch at the southwest edge of your range. Refrain from doing so and spread your men along the north edge of the Valley. A similar provision goes for you, Mr. Ditmar."

"Hmm!" said Fletcher. "So you figure them cows don't go west by way of the Valley?"

"They do not," Slade replied. "They go south across the Valley, on south a ways and then across the desert."

Fletcher stared. "You mean you figure the hellions know where there's water out there?" he demanded.

"Water, like gold, is where you find it," Slade

answered evasively. Ditmar shot him a quick and curious look but refrained from asking questions.

"Well, if you say to string the boys along the north edge of the Valley, that's what I'll do," said Fletcher. Ditmar again nodded agreement, without comment.

"You'll be doing the right thing if Slade says so," the sheriff put in.

"Got a notion you're plumb right, Brian," Fletcher agreed. "But what about Norman and Shaw?"

"Norman is already patrolling the south edge of his holding, tonight, and he's passing the word along to Shaw," Slade told them.

Ditmar spoke for the first time. "I assume you mean I should patrol where my holding ends to the south, Mr. Slade?"

"Exactly," El Halcon replied. "That way you should be able to intercept any stock that's being run in that direction."

"I see," Ditmar said thoughtfully. "Okay, I'll follow your advice, assiduously; I've a notion it will pay off. But suppose the devils catch on that we're patrolling that way?"

"Then," Slade said, with a slight smile, "it is logical to believe they will not attempt the run to the southwest; either way you stand to win."

"Makes sense," Ditmar conceded. "Okay, Mr. Slade, as I said, I'll follow your advice. The devil knows I can't trust my own judgment anymore, and when one can think of nothing, it's wise, I hold, to string along with somebody who can think of something."

John Fletcher nodded sober agreement.

A couple of quiet days followed. Nothing happened and El Halcon began to grow restless and uneasy. He felt sure the outlaws would strike somewhere, and soon, but where? That was the big question. The continual suspense was like waiting for the fellow upstairs to drop the other shoe. Sheriff Carter fumed and fussed. Slade wore a tranquil expression and did not comment. However, he was far from tranquil inside.

And then about mid morning of the third day, John Fletcher stormed in.

"They did it again!" he bellowed. "Run off a bunch of nearly a hundred from around a couple of waterholes on my north pasture."

"How, where?" demanded the sheriff.

"How in blazes do I know how or where!" snorted Fletcher. "We kept close watch along the north bank of the Canadian, up top the Valley, and never spotted a thing. Them cows just 'peared to vanish in thin air. Fact is, I'm just about ready to pull out—had about all I can take."

"Don't do it, Mr. Fletcher," Slade counseled earnestly. "Hang onto your land so long as you have a cow left."

"Uh-huh, that'll be just about it, one cow left," grunted Fletcher. "But I'll have something else left, too—a mortgage."

"A mortgage?"

"Uh-huh, Tobar Shaw talked me into it; he's a darn convincing talker when he takes a notion to be, and I'll have to admit what he had to say made sense. Young Brent of the JB said the same thing, but he ain't dry behind the ears yet and I didn't pay much attention to him. On the other hand, Shaw is a mature man of experience and should know what he's talking about. He showed me that the only way to meet the competition that's growin' up is to run in improved stock; he says the longhorns are on the way out and we might as well all face it."

"He's right there," Slade interpolated.

"So I figure," Fletcher conceded. "So I'm mortgaging the spread for money to buy the blankety-blank stock. Figure if we can just put a stop to the blankety-blank widelooping I should make out. But I won't be able to stand up against what's going on hereabouts now. And this section, as you know, is still kinda land poor—everybody got more acres than they really need, and the bank will be sorta chary about extensions and such. Case of meet your notes when they fall due or you're headed for trouble."

Which Slade knew very well was the truth.

"And Shaw gave you the advice," he remarked thoughtfully.

"Uh-huh, reckon he sorta tipped the balance," Fletcher admitted. "Us old fellers are hard to change, but we can see through the trunk of a tree if somebody chops a hole. What do you think, Slade?"

"I think," Slade said slowly, "that running in improved stock is wise, but I agree with you that the steady drain on your resources must stop. And you patrolled the north crest of the Valley carefully?"

"We did," Fletcher declared. "Nothing could have slipped through; had the boys strung out clear west to the edge of Shaw's holding, and it was a good bright night."

"I see," Slade said, the concentration furrow deepening between his black brows. "Okay, Mr. Fletcher, don't worry too much about the future. I venture to predict everything will shortly be cleared up and you will be satisfied that you have made a wise investment. Perhaps much wiser than you realize," he added cryptically.

Sheriff Carter shot him a quick look, but El Halcon did not see fit to amplify his last remark.

"Sure glad to hear you say it," said Fletcher. "You make me feel a helluva sight better. When you say something is so, I figure it's mighty apt to be so. Okay, let's amble over to the Trail End for a snort or two 'fore I head back to the spread."

As they walked, Slade turned to gaze northward, and the concentration furrow deepened a trifle more.

Fletcher's holding was peculiar in shape, like to a giant letter U laid on its side, the mouth or open end of the U pointing west. The south arm of the U, representing Fletcher's land south of the Canadian Valley, was shortened. The curve of the U swept around to the east and north and the northern arm was longer by many miles than the other, longer and wider. It represented Fletcher's holding to the north of the river and extended to Tobar Shaw's ranch to the west, which also included land north of the Valley.

Fletcher had his snorts and a sandwich, then hurried back to his casa, leaving Slade and Carter still at the table.

"Well, what do you think?" the latter asked.

"I think," Slade replied slowly, "that somebody made a slip, one that may well prove fatal for him; we'll discuss that later. Right now I'm going to pay the Valley and old Estaban a visit. This could prove the break we've been hoping for."

"Don't you think I'd better go along?" Carter suggested. Slade shook his head.

"No, I prefer to handle this one alone," he declined. "It's just in the nature of an exploring expedition. Be seeing you tomorrow, I hope."

The sheriff looked worried but did not argue the point, knowing it would be but a waste of time. Slade got the rig on Shadow and headed north by slightly west through the golden sunshine. Some distance from town he pulled up, as usual, and studied the back trail for a long time.

"I'd say we're not wearing a tail," he told Shadow. "Didn't think we would, but you never can tell. Anyhow, we won't take any unnecessary chances. We're up against a tough bunch with brains, feller, and *we* don't want to make a slip. Let's go!"

Chapter Twelve

Riding steadily, with the sun dipping westward, Slade reached the spot where the descent into the Valley was practicable. Again he sat for some minutes scanning the prairie in every direction. It stretched lonely and deserted for as far as the keen eyes of El Halcon could reach. Finally, confident that all was as it should be, he descended to the Valley floor and continued until he reached Estaban's lonely adobe, where he received a warm welcome. Estaban set forth a bountiful repast, to which they did full justice. Then, when cigarette and *cigaro* were drawing to their satisfaction, Estaban spoke.

"Knowing that *Capitan* would wish it, my *amigos* have watched the Valley, length and breadth," the old Mexican said. "*Capitan*, last night *ganado* crossed the Valley, far to the west."

Slade nodded, not looking particularly surprised. "Crossed and then headed south, I presume," he said.

"That is right, *Capitan*," Estaban replied. "After the stock had left the Valley, my *amigos* did not attempt to follow, knowing that on the open plain with the moon shining it would be unwise for them to do so."

"It certainly would have been," Slade agreed. "So the cows came from the north, crossed the Valley and headed south, far to the west of here."

"*Si*, far to the west of Tascosa; they did not pass Tascosa but entered the Valley far beyond, almost at the desert's edge."

"As I expected," Slade said musingly. "And now, Estaban, I have something to tell you. And what the ears hear, the heart keeps to itself."

"Assuredly, *Capitan*," Estaban replied, looking expectant.

Feeling that he had a right to know and confident he would keep a tight latigo on his jaw, Slade related the details of his discovery of the hidden water. Estaban listened with interest, but this time *he* did not appear particularly surprised.

"El Halcon sees all," he commented when Slade paused. "The *Indios* saw and understood, but even their eyes were not the eyes of El Halcon. What plan you to do with your discovery, *Capitan?*"

"Frankly, I don't know," Slade answered. "You have helped me a great deal tonight; you confirmed what I merely surmised. It may turn out to be highly important."

"It is the pleasure to be of assistance to El Halcon, the good, the just," returned Estaban. "My *amigos* will also be greatly pleased."

"They did a fine chore," Slade replied. "It is good to have friends."

"He who deserves friends always has friends," Estaban observed wisely. "When you call, *Capitan*, we will answer. Do you ride tonight?"

"Yes, I think I shall," Slade decided. "I want to have a good look at the northern slopes of the Valley, and I'll ride the Valley. If I mount to the prairie I'd be almost certain to run into some of Fletcher's hands patrolling, and I'd prefer not to. If my memory serves me, there is an old trail running close to the northern slopes, away from the plazas and not passing close to Tascosa."

"That is right," said Estaban. "It is a very old trail,

first beaten out by the *Indios*. In the old days, cattle thieves and Comanchero smugglers and other *ladrones* used it. Not much of a trail now, but it can be ridden."

"Then I'll take a chance on it," Slade replied. "I've a notion it will serve my purpose. I'll give my horse another hour of rest and then I'll move on."

Estaban broke out a bottle of wine and they had a drink together, then smoked and talked until the hour was up. Slade got the rig on his horse and set out. Shadow, rested and full of oats, was in the mood for an amble and stepped out briskly.

Fording without difficulty the river that at the moment was shallow, Slade rode straight across the Valley until he reached the old Indian track, which ran close to the northern slopes. He turned into the trail, now little more than a game track, and slowed the gait, studying the slopes with care. He knew there must be places where it was possible to descend without breaking a horse's leg or one's own neck, and he was anxious to spot them, although he did not believe they were much in use this far east.

Now the moon, just past the full, was well up in the sky and made the task easier. It was very lonely here, away from the plazas that as a rule hugged the river, and he doubted if the dwellers of the little settlements ever ventured far in this direction. The stillness was broken only by an occasional weird call of some night bird or the hauntingly beautiful distant plaint of a hunting wolf. Shadow's hoof beats sounded loud, rather louder than his master liked, but there was nothing much to do about it. It was unlikely, however, that there were any ears nearby to hear. But as he worked his way farther and farther west, he slowed the pace still more. Now it was well past midnight and he knew he was riding across Tobar Shaw's holding, the old Hartsook ranch which, like Fletcher's land, included pasture both to the south and the north of the Valley, although Hartsook had never used the north section much and presumably neither did Shaw, the once good market across the Oklahoma State Line now being nonexistent.

As he rode farther and farther west, Slade grew more alert, listening carefully to the calls of owls and other night birds and the yipping of coyotes. More than once the warning voices of those little friends had saved him from disaster; El Halcon knew the woodlands and their denizens as he knew the plains and the towns.

Right now he was taking no chances, for although he thought it unlikely, it was not beyond the realm of the possible that he might run into the wideloopers shoving another herd south. Didn't seem logical that they would raid two nights in succession, but they were a shrewd and unpredictable bunch and the unexpected appeared to be their forte.

The silence was deathly, with not a breath of wind stirring, but now and then a gold or scarlet leaf would drift slowly down through the still air to settle, with the tiniest of rustlings, amid its fellows for the long winter sleep. The subtle fingers of the frost were loosening their hold on the parent tree and the slightest vibration caused them to fall.

A slow mile slogged past, with only an occasional drifting leaf to break the monotony; and then he came to a point of ascent, wider than most and giving the appearance of having been traveled a good deal and recently. Slade drew rein, peering up its winding course.

"Feller, this looks like it," he said to Shadow. "Yes, I believe this is what we've been looking for."

He gave a final glance around. No sound other than the distant yipping of some coyotes broke the silence. Nowhere was there sign of motion other than that of a golden leaf which fanned his face with its fragrant breath. "Let's go, horse," he said, and put Shadow to the slope.

Riding slowly, straining his ears for any sound from above, he followed the winding track. He covered perhaps a third of the distance and rounded a sharp bend. And abruptly El Halcon realized he had ridden into a trap.

It wasn't much that warned him, just a sudden flutter of leaves from a stout tree branch under which he was passing, but it was enough. Instinctively he flung up his right arm to ward off a blow, and the tight loop snaking down from above slid along his forearm and missed its deadly strangle hold on his neck.

But the force of the instantly jerked rope hurled him from the saddle to strike the ground with stunning force.

A man slid down the tree trunk. Another followed. "Got him!" a voice exulted.

"We'll make sure," said another. A gun jutted forward.

From the prone figure on the ground gushed smoke and flame. Slade, although badly shaken by the shock of his fall, was shooting with both hands, rolling over and over as he pulled trigger. It was almost blind shooting, but at that distance El Halcon could hardly miss.

Answering slugs spatted the ground beside his moving body. Others fanned his face; then all at once he realized that only silence was coming through the swirling smoke cloud. He scrambled to his feet, both guns trained on the motionless forms lying on the ground.

Nothing more to fear from the pair of would-be killers, but he was still not in the clear, not by a long shot. On the prairie above, shouts were sounding, with answering cries from the Valley floor below, and a thudding of hoofs from both directions. A few more moments and he would be caught between deadly crossfire. The brush on either side of the track was more than usually dense and he could not hope to charge through it without giving away his position to the pursuers.

With frantic speed, he reloaded his guns, whipped into the saddle. His head was clearing, his hearing back to normal. Tense, ready, he strained his ears to the beat of hoofs loudening from below, estimated the distance; they were almost to the bend. His voice rang out—

"Trail, Shadow! Trail!"

The great black lunged forward, careened around the bend. He struck a horse shoulder to shoulder and knocked it off its feet, its rider catapulting into the brush. A second rider gave a howl of pain as both Slade's guns cut loose with a booming crash, whirled his mount and sent it plunging into the chaparral. Shadow sped on down the trail, rounded another bend. Slade drew a deep breath and holstered his guns. Now he was in the clear, with no chance of the pursuit catching up. Reaching the Valley floor, he swerved Shadow's head to the west.

"I'm going to find out what I came here to learn or know the reason why," he declared wrathfully, shaking his still-ringing head to free his brain of cobwebs.

"Keep going, horse, and keep your eyes peeled for some way up out of this blasted crack. That was a plumb smart try, and any other time of the year it would have been successful. But when that side-winder moved on the branch to drop his loop, he shook loose a bunch of autumn leaves and they told me he was up there. Yes, a smart try, and it'll take some puzzling to figure just how they handled it. I was absolutely certain I wasn't wearing a tail when I left town, but the obvious conclusion is that I was."

As he rode, he pondered the recent happening, trying to read the riddle of its planning. Quite possibly, he reasoned, his departure from Amarillo was noted and the smart devil heading the outfit surmised just what he had in mind and acted accordingly, very likely divining that he was in search of the way by which Fletcher's herd had been run across the Valley so far to the west. When he found it, it was plausible to believe he would ascend the slope to the prairie, which indeed he had in mind all the time. He had ridden slowly up the Valley and it would have been no trick for the outlaws to cut across and get ahead of him, avoiding Fletcher's patrols, which for horsemen would have posed little difficulty. Thus they would have had ample time to set their trap. Doubtless they had learned by bitter experience that trying to down El Halcon by way of an ortho-dox, run-of-mine dry-gulching was just a convenient way to commit suicide. Something unexpected and out of the ordinary was necessary were they to hope for success. Well, they had figured just that, and it had very nearly worked.

However, there was one weak angle where his reasoning was concerned. To all appearances he had been trailed along the old Indian track by the two devils who charged up the slope. And it seemed a trifle absurd to think they had so accurately foreseen his movements. Of course they could have been concealed near where the way up the slope from the valley floor began, keeping at a discreet distance until the shooting on the slope intimated he had blundered into the trap, then hightailing to be in on the kill.

More likely, he believed, they had entered the Valley by the same route as he had and had lain hidden some distance from Estaban's cabin and had seen him leave the adobe and head straight across the Valley. Then they would have known he was making for the old trail near the north slopes and, keeping well to the rear, had followed.

It was all conjecture, of course, but that could also be the explanation.

If that were so, he wondered a bit uneasily if the hellions might attempt to take vengeance on Estaban. It seemed rather unlikely, however—Estaban was a tough old jigger, with his repeating rifle always at hand. The windows of his adobe were barred, the doors double-locked, the thick walls impervious to gunfire. And he had many friends in the Valley who kept watch over him, able to move like an Indian in the chaparral with ready rifle. Just the same, he'd keep the possibility in mind.

He had covered quite a few miles before he discovered what he sought, a negotiable way up the slopes to the prairie. It proved to be rather tough going, but Shadow made it, with the expenditure of a few disgusted snorts and blowings. On the crest, Slade drew rein and sat gazing southward across the Valley.

"You're a smart jigger, all right, Mr. Tobar Shaw,"

he apostrophized the Bradded H owner. "Can't say as I ever contacted a smarter. You had me completely fooled for quite a while; I hardly gave you a thought. Undoubtedly you are a master at covering up, keeping always in the background, unobtrusive, self-effacing, just a respectable ranch owner with a modest holding. Yes, you were plumb smart, until you made the slip of running Fletcher's cows across your holding, the only route by which the patrolling hands could be avoided. The little slip the outlaw brand always makes, sooner or later. And inducing Fletcher to mortgage his spread tightened the loop just a little more. I wonder if you are enough of a geologist to have read the signs aright? Looks a little that way. Well, we'll see about that later.

"Also you are a master of the unexpected. Well, right now I aim to employ a little unexpected-pulling myself."

Upon which he rode east at a fast pace, heading for the descent where the trap had been set. It was highly unlikely that the outlaws had remained in the vicinity—no reason for them to do so—and anyhow, on the open prairie he had nothing to fear from them. Also, he felt confident they would not expect him to return to the scene.

Without misadventure, he reached the point of descent and rode boldly down it. He wanted a look at the bodies of the two outlaws.

In that, however, he was doomed to disappointment; the bodies were nowhere to be found. Evidently they had been loaded onto the horses the pair must have ridden and carried off.

"Which means, I'd say," he remarked to Shadow, "that they were a couple of Shaw's cowhands and would have been recognized by somebody as such.

Well, guess we'd better head for Estaban's shack. Be long past daylight by the time we get there."

It was, and both horse and man were pretty well worn out; it had been an exhausting night.

Estaban took a look at him, asked no questions and motioned to the comfortable bunk in his little spare room, where Slade had slept before. The Ranger did not argue the point and tumbled into bed without delay, knowing Estaban would properly care for Shadow.

Chapter Thirteen

It was past mid afternoon when he awoke, still a bit sore from his tumble of the night before but otherwise his normal self and much refreshed. While he ate his breakfast, he recounted his adventure on the slope and his conclusions relative to Tobar Shaw, mentioning, too, his apprehension lest the outlaws, did they know of his visit to the adobe, might seek to retaliate by harming Estaban.

The old Mexican's lined face grew grim. "Have not the fear on that score, *Capitan*," he replied. "I myself can care for, and besides I have *amigos* who know and watch. None can my adobe approach with evil intent and live." Slade believed it.

"Well, at least I now know whom to keep an eye on, which is a lot more than I knew this time last week," he observed.

"The eye of El Halcon sees all," said Estaban.

As he rode to Amarillo, Walt Slade did some hard thinking. It was all very well to be convinced that Tobar Shaw was the head of the outlaw bunch which had been terrorizing the section, but proving it was something else again. He was forced to admit that he had not a scintilla of proof against Shaw that would stand up in court. So far, the Bradded H owner had kept absolutely in the clear. Confronted with the charge that the stolen cows had passed over his holding to reach the desert crossing, Shaw could come forward with any number of plausible explanations:

he had mistakenly stationed his patrols too far to the east; some of his men had been sick—he employed less than a dozen—and those fit for duty could not efficiently cover so wide an area, etc.

All of which meant that he, Slade, had to get his slippery quarry dead to rights. How? He hadn't the slightest notion, at the moment. Meanwhile, Shaw was free to commit some other depredation, which Slade gravely feared might be more lethal than cow stealing.

What would it be? Again he had no idea. Perhaps a talk with Sheriff Carter might help. He quickened Shadow's pace.

Sheriff Carter listened with absorbed interest to Slade's account of the night's happenings, but when the Ranger expressed his conviction that Tobar Shaw was the head of the outlaw organization, the old peace officer's reaction of astonishment bordered on incredulity.

"If you'd said Ditmar, I wouldn't be so dadblamed flabbergasted," he protested. "But Shaw! Never gave him a thought."

"The same went for me until there was no doubt but that Fletcher's cows were driven across his land," Slade replied. "Then I began thinking seriously about Shaw. He's a smooth hombre, all right, with brains he knows how to use."

"You don't suppose it could have been a bunch Shaw had nothing to do with that really managed to avoid his patrols?" the sheriff asked. Slade shook his head.

"I took that into consideration," he replied, "until that elaborate, carefully planned, and skillfully executed attempt to do away with me there on the slope. Was largely just luck it didn't succeed."

"Rather, your ability to think like a lightning flash," the sheriff interpolated.

"Possibly," Slade conceded, "although I hold that luck played a part. As I told Shadow, any other time of year they would have put it across. Remember, it was definitely admitted that the cows were run across the Valley by way of a far western route. An outlaw bunch would have known that and that there would be nothing to be gained from endeavoring to protect that route. In my opinion, Shaw realized I was catching on and made a desperate attempt to get rid of me before I passed my conclusions to others."

"I see," said Carter. "You sure make a case against him, all right. Were it anybody else doing the talking I'd still be a mite dubious, but if you say it, I reckon it's so. By the way, do you figure he's caught on that you discovered the hidden water?"

"That I'm inclined to doubt," Slade replied. "I'm of the opinion that he doesn't believe I have the necessary know-how to figure that out. Otherwise, I'd say he would have hesitated to run that last herd south and across the desert. Very likely, did he believe I had discovered the water, he would probably presume that I would have laid a trap for him at the edge of the desert or along the dry wash. In fact, I would have, had I not feared I'd only bag a few hired hands, with Shaw in the clear. And dropping a loop on him is my most important chore."

Again the sheriff agreed. "And you figure he may turn to something else and drop the cow stealing for a while?"

"That's what I fear," Slade admitted. "I'm beating my brains out trying to anticipate what he has in mind, so far with no success. If we could just get the jump on him there'd be a good chance to get rid of the pest."

For some moments, Slade was silent, his eyes gazing through the open window toward the far distances.

"There's something else I'm wondering about," he said. "Because of Shaw's concentrating his wide-looping activities on Fletcher's spread. He seems intent on forcing Fletcher into a position where he'll be forced to either sell his holding or lose it."

"And what does that mean?" asked Carter.

"I am firmly convinced," Slade replied, "that to the northeast of here will be developed the greatest oil and natural gas field in Texas, perhaps in the world, and a portion of it will be under Fletcher's land. The surface slope of the area, very slight, is from northeast to southwest. But far down in the earth, hundreds, perhaps thousands of feet, the slope is reversed, trending from southwest to northeast; the petrological outcroppings in the Canadian River Valley prove that conclusively, which would mean that oil drainage would be from the southwest, and there are plenty of indications that a vast oil and gas pool is below the surface, doubtless very far below. Eventually Fletcher's land will be worth a fortune. Up to the present the oil men have concentrated on the Beaumont field and those to the south of Houston and south of Laredo. They have paid the Panhandle country very little mind because of inadequate transportation facilities. That, however, is fast being remedied, with the railroads pushing steadily to the west. Soon their attention will be focused on northwest Texas, and development will follow. The petroleum industry is growing by leaps and bounds and soon such oil tycoons as Gates, Rockefeller, Hogg, and others will be on the search for new production fields and will turn to northwest Texas."

"Hmm!" the sheriff remarked thoughtfully, "as it happens I own a little strip over there myself, east of Brent's holding."

"Hang onto it," Slade counseled. "It will make you rich in your old age."

"Then it had better get busy darn fast," grunted Carter. "I'm already hearing the 'old hound' baying on my trail."

"Oh, you'll last to be a hundred," Slade consoled him. "Yes, right here is going to be an oil and gas production that'll make folks sit up and take notice."

Future events were to prove El Halcon right in every detail.

"This whole area was, of course," Slade continued, "once a great inland sea or lake, with conditions ideal for the manufacture of petroleum, and the slow, subtle chemistry of nature, working through untold ages, did just that.

"So getting back to what all this prefaced, I'm wondering if Tobar Shaw has also read aright conditions prevailing here and is playing for much bigger stakes than widelooping and robbery."

"Meaning that if he can get Fletcher into enough difficulties so he'll be forced to sell or can't meet his notes, the bank would take over the holding and Shaw would bid it in," the sheriff observed shrewdly.

"Exactly," Slade agreed. "I'll admit that I wondered a little about Ditmar when he expressed a desire to acquire Keith Norman's land, but knew that if he had an inkling as to conditions, he had guessed wrong, there being no oil under Norman's holding, the seepage that formed the pool being to the northeast. But after talking with him, I concluded he didn't have the necessary knowledge and was truthful when he said he merely wished to extend his holdings. And he just didn't fit into the picture right. The devious manner in which the various depredations were committed was totally at variance with his impulsive, forthright nature; his methods would be direct, and much easier to cope with."

"Guess that's so," admitted Carter. "Now that you point it out, I can see it, too. He's a brawler and a trouble maker when he has a few snorts under his belt, but I reckon that's all.

"Blast it!" he added, "I just can't get over the way the hellions tried to do for you in the Valley. Of all the snake-blooded things, and plumb unexpected, too, wasn't it?"

"It was," Slade answered. "It evinced understanding and careful planning. There's nothing new about dropping a strangle-noose over an unwary rider's head, from a tree branch, but the manner in which that try was made verged on the unique. They didn't try it in the Valley below, because there it was logical to believe a rider would be keeping a close watch on his surroundings, but on the slope it was natural to expect his attention would be directed to the trail ahead, which indeed happened to be the case. And having those units posted above and below the slope to take over in case the nice little attempt at hanging happened not to work out—that was original. What the devils didn't count on was Shadow and what would happen to anything that got in his way when he really meant business. And when he knocked that cayuse heels over tincup and pitched his rider into the brush, the other hellion decided he didn't want any part of him and also hightailed into the chaparral."

"Especially with blue whistlers buzzin' all around him," the sheriff commented dryly.

"And I'm pretty sure I nicked him, from the way he yelped," Slade added. "Yes, it was a nice try, but it didn't work, and that's all that counts."

"Guess that's right," agreed Carter. "Well, suppose we drop over to the Trail End for a bite; all this palaver makes me hungry."

As they entered the saloon and occupied a table, Carter exclaimed: "Look, there's the hellion now, standing at the bar. I'd never have in a month of Sundays figured him for what he is. Looks like butter wouldn't melt in his blasted mouth."

"Outward appearances are often deceptive," Slade replied. "There is a keen and ruthless brain back of that placid and quite ordinary countenance. And notice his moves, assured, without hesitancy. His hand goes to its objective without a hint of fumbling. The mark of an able and adroit man."

"I sure wish I could see things like you do," sighed the sheriff. "You never seem to miss a bet, and when you point out something, it stands out as plain as a cowpoke in church. Easy to spot as a hole through a grindstone. I don't know how you do it."

"Training," Slade smiled.

"Uh-huh, training, and eyes that see what everybody else passes over," said Carter.

While he ate, Slade studied the Bradded H owner. Shaw did indeed appear perfectly composed, not at all perturbed over the failure of his cunningly conceived scheme for murder the night before, which had entailed the loss of two of his followers and the wounding of a third. Abruptly he placed his empty glass precisely in the middle of the bar and walked out with his lithe, assured stride. Turning, he glanced toward the table and waved a cordial goodnight; Slade waved back. The sheriff muttered under his breath.

"That wind spider is up to something," he vowed. "I can feel it in my bones."

"Very likely," Slade concurred. "But what? That's the question to which I would very much like to have an answer."

Carter pushed back his empty plate and stuffed his pipe with tobacco. "Think I'll go to bed shortly," he announced. "How about you?"

"Not just yet," Slade replied. "I didn't get up until afternoon and I'm not sleepy. Think I'll browse around a bit."

"Okay, but watch your step," cautioned the sheriff. "Next time you may not have a shower of autumn leaves to put you hep to what's in the wind."

"Perhaps I should have brought one along as a good luck piece," Slade smiled. Carter grunted, and puffed on his pipe. Abruptly he sat up in his chair.

"Hey!" he exclaimed, "what's all this?"

Chapter Fourteen

Men were filing through the swinging doors. They were not dressed as cowhands but wore overalls, open-neck shirts and laced boots that were mud-stained. Fully two dozen crowded to the bar and ordered drinks.

"What in blazes!" the sheriff varied his exclamation. "Who are those fellers? I never saw them before."

He found out a moment later when Swivel-eye Sanders hurried over and dropped into a chair.

"Figured it was going to be a quiet night, but it ain't," said Swivel-eye. "See those jiggers? I just got the word. They're railroad builders. Understand the railroad is going to expand the yards and about a hundred of the hellions rolled into town just a little while ago—a whole trainload of 'em."

"Blazes!" the sheriff repeated. "I was told that work wouldn't start till after the first of next week."

"So I heard, too," said Swivel-eye. "But it seems the company is in a hurry to get the work started and to-morrow is those jiggers' payday, so they rushed 'em to town so they could have their bust and get on the job. Seems a lot of 'em are starting to celebrate early. Paycar is in the yards but won't start handing out the *dinero* until morning; then things will really hum."

"I see," said the sheriff. "Understand those hellions have been working out on the line to the east and I reckon they haven't been in town since before last payday and are already pretty well heeled. You'll do business tonight, Swivel, and so will the other rumholes." He knocked out his pipe and stood up.

"Where you goin', Brian?" Swivel asked.

"Where am I going!" snorted the sheriff. "I'm going to round up my deputies and swear in two or three specials; figure I'll need 'em 'fore the night's over. Dadblame it! no sleep for me tonight. How about you, Walt?"

"I'll wait here until you return," Slade answered.

"Okay," said Carter. "Oh, why did I ever get in this sheriffin' business!" he lamented. "Never a minute's peace!"

"He's a darned old liar," chuckled Swivel, one eye jovial, the other leering as they followed the sheriff's progress to the swinging doors. "Pertends to have his bristles up over what's happened, but the truth is he just dotes on excitement. Let two or three days without anything happening go past and he gets as restless as a dog sittin' on a cactus. I'll send over a drink."

"Make it coffee," Slade said.

"Okay," replied Swivel. He motioned to a waiter and hurried back to the far end of the bar.

Another bunch of railroad builders rolled in and were greeted with hilarious shouts from the first arrivals. Business in the Trail End was picking up, and fast.

After a while the sheriff reappeared, still scowling but with a gleam in his eye that belied his doleful expression.

"Well, I've got 'em scattered over town keeping a watch on things," he announced as he slumped into a chair opposite Slade who, as usual, sat where he could keep an eye on the windows and the swinging doors. "There'll be trouble down around the lake before the night is over. You just watch. The gals there and the card sharps will be out to take those fellers over, and they look to me like a salty bunch that won't stand for much nonsense."

Slade was inclined to agree; the railroad builders certainly didn't appear to be all sweetness and light, and after a month or more of slogging along the right-of-way across the lonely prairie, they doubt-less craved diversion.

After a couple of drinks, the sheriff hurried off to see how his deputies were making out. Slade stayed on at the table, sipping coffee and pondering what Swivel-eye had said; an idea was building up in his mind.

The night wore on, with the turmoil in the Trail End increasing as the redeye got in its licks. The railroad builders were noisy and hilarious, but Slade did not believe there was any real harm in them. Just a hardy bunch of honest workers out to have a good time. Now and then arguments devel-oped, but Swivel and his floor men quickly restored peace.

Abruptly Slade stood up. He waved to Swivel and sauntered out. The street was also quite crowded, for the word of the excitement had gotten around and the citizens of Amarillo, always looking for an excuse to raise heck, were joining in. Slade chuckled and headed for the Washout and the lake front.

When he reached the Washout, he found it also doing a good business. Thankful Yates greeted him hilariously, asked about Jerry Norman and insisted they have a drink together.

"Those railroad fellers are scattered all around," he remarked as they sat down. "Not a bad bunch, I'd say. Sorta rough and ready but all right. The gals

seem to take to 'em, and that is always a good sign."
He paused to sip his drink.

"Some jiggers in a little while ago I didn't particular care for," he continued. "Salty-looking hellions, four of 'em. 'Peared to be watching for somebody. Cowhands, I reckon, they were dressed that way. Didn't stay long. We get all sorts here, you know, and I'm usually purty quick at spotting the wrong kind. Somehow those four didn't strike me as being just right. Could be mistaken, though. Behaved themselves all right. Had a coupla drinks apiece and then moseyed out. Nope, I never saw them before."

"How long since they left?" Slade asked.

"Oh, about half an hour, I reckon," Thankful replied. "They didn't stay long. Say, things are hoppin' for fair; I'll have to get back to the bar."

He rolled away with his peculiar, almost sailor-like gait. Slace wondered if the transplanted New Englander had once been a sailor. Not likely. Anyhow, he was all right and a square shooter.

The Washout was booming, no doubt as to that, and Slade enjoyed the hilarity. But he couldn't keep his mind on what was going on. Somehow Thankful's discourse on the four men he deemed unsavory kept intruding on his thoughts.

"Blast it," he muttered. "I'm going to play a hunch. May be plumb loco, but I can't help but feel it isn't." With a final glance around, he waved to Thankful and departed. Without hesitation, he headed for the railroad station at First Avenue and Pierce Street. Arriving at the station, he entered and accosted the night agent, with whom he was acquainted.

"Sam," he said, after they had exchanged greetings, "just where is the paycar located? I understand they pay off tomorrow morning."

The agent's eyes widened a little. "Why, on that spur over to the west, not far from the lake," he replied. "Something wrong, Mr. Slade?"

"Frankly, I don't know," the Ranger answered. "I'm just sort of playing a hunch. Be seeing you later." He walked out, leaving the agent looking concerned.

It was some little distance to the yards and Slade walked swiftly. Here there were very few people on the streets and the lighting was inadequate, so El Halcon was very much on the alert, frequently glancing over his shoulder. However, he saw nothing that could be termed alarming and reached the yards without incident.

At this point the yards were silent and lonely. At the far end, a couple of switch engines chugged about cheerfully, signal lights turned, couplers clashed, brake rigging jangled, but here there was a lack of activity, the darkness relieved only by the wan glow of the low-lying switch lights. Slade surveyed the scene a moment, then moved on, carefully avoiding the feeble beams of the switch lights, until the bulk of the lighted paycar loomed before him, and beyond it a street.

Again he paused, then glided cautiously toward the car; now the hunch was going strong, and the soundless monitor in his brain was voicing a warning. He slowed his pace, reached the car. Inside the slightly open door he could hear a mutter of voices and a rustling sound. He peered through the door crack, got a glimpse of what was going on inside and flung the door wide open.

The paymaster and the paycar guard sat rigid in chairs; two men stood with guns trained on them. Two more men were squatting beside an open safe, transferring its contents to a canvas sack. Slade's voice rang out—

"Elevate! You're covered! In the name of the law—"

The men at the safe leaped erect, the other two whirled to face Slade. The car rocked to a bellow of gunfire.

Weaving, ducking, slithering, Slade shot with both hands. A slug gashed the flesh of his left arm, another tore through the leg of his overalls. One of the robbers slumped to the floor, a second rocked on his heels and fell backward. The two remaining trained their guns on the moving Ranger.

Chapter Fifteen

But now the plucky guard, a former card dealer, was in action. His right hand darted forward, a stubby little double-barreled derringer spatted into his palm and boomed like thunder. One of the outlaws went down, the other glanced toward the report and the second barrel of the derringer tore half his face off.

Slade heard a sound outside the car and went sideways in a convulsive leap as a gun blazed from the darkness. His Colts let go twice. Thumbs hooked over the hammers, he held his fire an instant, heard a clatter of hoofs on the nearby street, fading into the distance, and began replacing the spent shells with fresh cartridges.

"The blankety-blank got away!" the guard bawled indignantly.

"Yes, and I've a notion he was the he-wolf of the pack," Slade replied. "Well, anyhow we did a pretty good chore of mopping up," he added, glancing at the still forms sprawled on the floor.

"I was hoping and praying I'd get a chance to use my sleeve gun," said the guard. "They cleaned my holster, of course, but I guess they never thought of my derringer. Anyway, they overlooked it."

"And you sure got a chance to use it at just the right time," Slade replied. "The odds were a mite lopsided. Now suppose you hustle across town and locate the sheriff. Chances are he'll be at the Trail End, awaiting me. If he isn't, look in his office."

"Okay," said the guard and hurried out. Slade turned to the elderly paymaster, who still sat rigid in his chair, white to the lips. Evidently he was not used to such bloody doings. Slade's quiet, musical voice seemed to relax him.

"Now suppose you tell me just what happened," he suggested. "How did those horned toads get the drop on you?"

"I was working on the payroll," the other replied. "The guard was sitting beside me. All of a sudden we heard what seemed to be somebody tapping on the window over there. Naturally we both looked in that direction. Those four devils crashed in the door and, as you cowboys say, caught us settin'; we couldn't do a thing."

"Fortunate that you didn't try to," Slade said. He glanced at the safe and the bulging sack on the floor.

"Would have made a pretty nice haul, eh?" he remarked.

"Yes, they sure would have," replied the paymaster. "Not only are we paying off here tomorrow but there's money, too, for Tucumcari. You saved my company a lot, sir; they'll have something to say to you. Yes, there'll be a nice reward coming your way."

"The chance to be of service was reward enough," Slade answered.

"And I've a strong notion, sir, that you saved Potter, the guard, and myself from being murdered," the paymaster added, with a shudder. "Those devils struck me as the sort not to leave witnesses."

"You could be right," Slade conceded. In fact, he thought it quite likely, especially if Shaw had used some of his cowhands for the chore; he'd find out about that later.

"Listen!" the paymaster suddenly exclaimed.

"Somebody's coming." He glanced nervously at the door.

"The boys from the other end of the yard, the chances are," Slade said as he sat down and began manufacturing a cigarette. "They must have heard the shooting and are coming to investigate."

Shouts were sounding outside, and the pad of hurrying feet. Another moment and the car was filled with excited trainmen volleying questions.

The paymaster answered, stressing the part Slade had played. Somebody suddenly shouted—

"Why, it's Mr. Slade, Sheriff Carter's new deputy! Been hearing plenty about him. You sure did a good chore here, Mr. Slade. If the hellions had got away with what's in the safe, we'd have all died of thirst tomorrow."

A general laugh followed the sally. Appreciative glances were cast at Slade.

"Don't forget the part the guard played," Slade reminded them. "He sure got into action at just the right time."

"Uh-huh, John Potter is okay, and a salty hombre," observed a conductor.

"Don't touch the bodies," Slade warned. "I want the sheriff to see them as they are. He should be along shortly. By the way, take a good look, though, and see if you've ever seen them before."

The trainmen peered at the dead faces and one and all shook their heads.

"Nope, never clapped eyes on the sidewinders before," said the conductor. "Ornery looking hellions. Well, they got just what was coming to them. Here's the sheriff."

Potter, the guard, and the old peace officer strode in, two deputies trailing after them. Carter bent over and scanned the bodies, glanced at Slade and shook his head.

"All right, boys," the conductor said to his companions, "back on the job. Work to do if we hope to take it easy tomorrow night. Much obliged again, Mr. Slade, you're a real hombre."

They strode out, waving their *adios*. The sheriff began turning out the outlaws' pockets, revealing nothing of importance save plenty of money, which he confiscated for the county treasury. Slade examined the seams.

"More alkali dust," he announced. "They've all been out on the desert; part of the widelooping bunch, all right."

"They'd have done better by themselves to have stayed there," grunted Carter. His gaze fixed on Slade, who was sopping up the blood that trickled down onto his hand from his bullet-creased arm.

"And you for a visit to Doc Beard," he said as he inspected the outlaws' guns.

"Reg'lation artillery," he reported. "Wonder how about their horses? Should be around somewhere close."

"I think they followed the hellion who got away," Slade replied. "Not sure, though."

"Take a look, Hartley," the sheriff ordered his saturnine chief deputy. "We'll have these carcasses moved out of your way, pronto," he told the paymaster. "I'm going to leave one of my deputies with you, just in case. Right, Walt?"

"I doubt if there will be an encore, but best not to take chances," the Ranger concurred. "It's an unpredictable bunch, and we don't know how many more might be waiting around somewhere."

"And I'm taking up my post outside, where I can

see in all directions," declared Potter. "I craves peace and quiet for the rest of the night."

The chief deputy returned to report no trace of the horses, which did not surprise Slade.

"Take a look at the rumholes while you're here," Carter told him. "Cal, you stay in the car."

As they headed for Doc Beard's office, Slade remarked, "Thought it just possible you might recognize the devils as some of Shaw's cowhands."

"I didn't," Carter replied. "Ain't over surprising, though, seems they never come to Amarillo, except a couple that sometimes accompanies him when he visits town, always the same two. I've gathered the rest of them do their drinking at Tascosa, can't even say for sure about that. Seems nobody knows anything much about them, not even Keith Norman, their neighbor to the east. Oh, he's a shrewd one, no doubt about that. Say, how in blazes did you catch on to what was in the wind tonight?"

"I didn't," Slade admitted. "I just played a hunch. You know we've been beating our brains out trying to figure what Shaw might pull next. All of a sudden it came to me that the paycar would make a nice haul. And Thankful Yates had mentioned four questionable looking characters visiting his place and appearing to be watching for somebody. So, as I said, I played a hunch."

"And, as usual, the hunch, as you call it, was just another case of going over all the angles and adding 'em up correctly. Well, here's Doc's office and there's a light burning; the old coot never seems to sleep. Come on, I want him to look you over."

Personally, Slade paid the light wound no mind, but went along with Carter, to relieve his anxiety.

Doc Beard thought little of it, too. He cleansed the

slight cut and applied a couple of strips of plaster, to the accompaniment of a running fire of caustic remarks.

"Out!" he concluded. "I crave shuteye. Yes, I'll hold an inquest tomorrow, two o'clock; just a waste of time. Out!"

"And now what's next?" asked the sheriff, when they were on the street.

"I figure the Trail End and a cup of coffee won't go bad," Slade decided.

"And I can stand a snort or two before going to bed," said Carter. "Things were quieting down when I left. Guess the boys have got rid of most of their spare change and are feeling a mite tuckered. They'll be there with bells on tomorrow night, though. Heard forty or fifty more will roll in before morning. The Division Superintendent was in and told me he doesn't figure on anything much tomorrow except getting the camp cars in shape, and they'll be rarin' to go."

The Trail End crowd had pretty well dispersed, the dance-floor girls and the orchestra were gone, and Swivel-eye was getting ready to politely request the diehards to get the blankety-blank hell outa there. Slade had his coffee, the sheriff his drinks and both headed for bed, the Ranger quite pleased with the day's work. With the able assistance of John Potter, the paycar guard, he had managed to eliminate four more of the outlaw band and felt that Shaw might be running out of hired hands.

Of course a leader of his proven ability could enlist replacements, but not likely of the same calibre as the members of his original outfit whom Slade believed to have been chosen for ruthlessness and intelligence. Well, things weren't going so bad, although his main objective would not be achieved until he eliminated, one way or another, the shadowy head of the bunch.

Yes, Tobar Shaw was a shadow. As elusive a hellion as El Halcon had ever locked horns with. Oh, well, he had gone up against somewhat similar rapscallions, to their disadvantage. He went to bed and slept soundly.

The inquest was much the same as the former one. Slade and John Potter were warmly praised for doing an excellent chore. The four vinegaroons got exactly what was coming to them. Plant 'em and forget 'em!

Thankful Yates, who had attended the inquest, drew Slade aside. "They were the four hellions I told you about," said the Washout owner. "The ones I said I didn't like the looks of."

"So I judged," Slade replied. "And you say they didn't talk to anybody while in the Washout?"

"That's right," answered Thankful. "Though, as I said, they 'peared to be sorta on the lookout for somebody. Maybe you?"

"Could have been, though I rather doubt it," Slade conceded. "Well, your estimate of them was confirmed."

"In the likker business you sorta get so you can pick 'em," said Thankful. "Be seeing you. Hope you bring Miss Jerry Norman in soon; I like her."

"Wouldn't be surprised if I do," Slade said. "In fact, I've got a feeling she might show up in town today. Young Joyce Echols was in the Trail End for a little while last night, Sheriff Carter said, and he'd tell about the bust due for tonight. That is quite likely to bring in old Keith and Jerry; they sort of take to payday busts."

"Be seeing you," Thankful repeated and headed back to his place.

Once again Slade spent some hours sauntering about town in the hope of learning something significant, and did not.

Meanwhile in the railroad yards, gold was flowing from the paycar in a Pactolian stream, be it permitted to compare that prosaic conveyance to the fabled river whose sands were reputed to consist of the precious metal. Anyhow, plenty of *dinero* was being handed out and the saloons and other entertainment spots were preparing to reap the harvest.

And very likely, Slade feared, there would be trouble before the night was over. Such establishments as the Trail End and the Washout were run strictly on the up-and-up and managed to keep order or something resembling it. But there were other places of dubious reputation, to put it mildly, where anything could happen and usually did.

Which gave the Ranger food for thought. Such conditions might well provide opportunity for gentlemen of the Tobar Shaw brand.

Sheriff Carter was of a like opinion, and worried. "I've got five specials swore in, but there's a lot of territory to cover," he said. Slade nodded in sober agreement.

The day jogged along in green and gold and sunwashed air. Already the streets and the drinking places were crowded. Cowhands who had heard about the bust were riding in to take part in the celebration. The business people were also in a holiday mood, knowing that the payday bust for the railroaders was just a forerunner to the added prosperity the big job of expanding the yards would bring. Amarillo was all set to stand up on her hind legs and howl.

At present it was a jovial howl of excitement, pleasure and good fellowship. Later, after the dark closed down it would very likely take on a sinister note, a lethal whine rising to a screech, raucous and deadly. Such was usually the case in any frontier town when quick-tempered young men fared forth with weapons at their belts.

And far to the west, four men rode purposefully as they headed for the Cowboy Capital on a mission of vengeance.

Chapter Sixteen

The object of said mission, had he been aware of what they had in mind, would not have been particularly perturbed, being confident of his ability to cope with any such attempt. Slade enjoyed a leisurely dinner in the crowded Trail End and conferred with Sheriff Carter. His prediction to Thankful Yates proved correct and while they were talking, old Keith Norman rolled in with Jerry in tow.

"Heard about the doin's here tonight and she pestered me into bringing her in," he said to Slade. "I told her you'd be too busy to be cluttered up with females, but she wouldn't listen."

"I expect I'll be able to spare her a minute or two," El Halcon smiled as he pulled out a chair. "Peaceful enough here, so far, save for a lot of noise."

"Lot of noise is right," grunted Norman as he sat down. "Those railroad fellers have voices like locomotive whistles and they sure believe in using 'em. Waiter!"

After finishing their drinks, Norman and the sheriff moved to the bar for a word with acquaintances, leaving Slade and Jerry alone at the table.

"Now tell me what all has happened since I saw you last," the girl said. "Don't hold back anything, dear, for you know sometimes I can help you."

He told her everything, including his conviction that Tobar Shaw was the head of the outlaw bunch. Jerry did not appear particularly surprised.

"Somehow I never liked him," she said. "Courteous and well spoken as he is. Why I don't know—call it a woman's intuition, if you will, I just don't. Whereas Mr. Ditmar, who is what I suppose you would call a rough-and-ready sort, I do like. He strikes me as being honest and sincere. I know Sheriff Carter has always been a bit suspicious of him, but I didn't go along with that."

"He is honest and sincere," Slade interpolated. "Sort of has a chip on his shoulder and is inclined to get rough if provoked, but completely trustworthy."

"So I figured him," Jerry said. "When he was at our place we got him to talking about himself a little. Told us how his parents died when he was very young and how he was reared by a shiftless old uncle who also died, when he was fourteen. How he worked at odd jobs to support himself, became a cowhand, and saved his money. Frankly admitted that he won a good deal of it at cards. Anyhow accumulated enough to buy his spread. Appears to be ambitious and wants to get ahead."

"He will," Slade predicted. "His sort usually does. If some good woman can just get hold of him I feel pretty sure he'll make a go at it."

"Don't be hinting," Jerry giggled. "I'm not interested that way, as you very well know. Though I suppose if one can't have the moon, one should be satisfied with sixpence, as the saying goes. Oh, well, even though you can't hold the moon, it's nice to have it shine on you now and then. Disappears for a while, but always comes back.

"And now I have something to tell you, dear," she added seriously. "Late this afternoon, Shaw and three men rode this way. We saw them as we rode down the trail from the casa. I'm sure they were headed for Amarillo, although we did not see them again. I thought you'd like to know."

"You're right," he replied. "And it may be of help. At least I can pretty well count on the hellion being in town tonight. Thanks for telling me."

"But those terrible men being in town may mean danger for you," she worried.

"Forewarned is forearmed," he returned lightly. "I don't think there's anything to bother about."

Suddenly a thought struck him. "By the way, do you think Shaw saw you and Uncle Keith headed for town?" he asked.

"He could hardly have missed seeing us riding from the ranchhouse to the trail," she replied. "However, they speeded up right after they passed us and we didn't overtake them. Why?"

"Just wondering," he evaded. She regarded him doubtfully but did not question him further.

"Going to take me to the Washout tonight?" she asked.

He hesitated, that disturbing thought working in his mind. Oh, the devil! She'd be as safe one place as another and they had plenty of friends in the Washout.

"Okay, if you wish me to," he agreed. "A little later. Hadn't you better have something to eat?"

"I could stand a bite," she admitted. "Have coffee with me."

Slade summoned a waiter and gave the order. He smoked and sipped his coffee while she ate.

Norman and the sheriff approached. "We're going over to Tumulty's place for a little while," the latter announced. "You going to stick around here?"

"We're going down to the Washout a little later,"
Slade replied. Carter shot him a sharp look and his
brows drew together.

"All right," he said. "Chances are I'll see you there."

Now the Trail End was really beginning to hop.
The bar was crowded and so was the dance floor.
Every table was occupied. The roulette wheels spun
merrily. The musicians fiddled madly. There were
bursts of song, or what was apparently intended
for it, and a constant bumble of loud-voiced conversation.

Jerry's eyes were sparkling, her cheeks flushed. "I
like it," she said, "and I'll bet the Washout is even
livelier." Slade thought that very likely it was, and he
experienced a slight qualm of uneasiness over his
ready acquiescence to her request to take her to the
lake-front place. Thankful Yates usually kept pretty
good order, but the Washout was frequented by a
rougher crowd than was generally to be found at the
Trail End. Trouble could cut loose there. Oh, well,
they'd make out.

Jerry finished her dinner and glanced suggestively at her table companion.

"Shall we go?" she said. "I expect Joyce Echols and
some more of the boys will be there; they like the
Washout, too."

Slade was more than usually watchful as they
threaded their way through the crowd on the streets,
for it was fairly obvious that Tobar Shaw and his
three henchmen were somewhere in town. And that
disturbing thought still persisted, based on the fact
that Shaw very probably knew Jerry liked the Washout and would doubtless inveigle him into taking
her there. But as he said, forewarned was forearmed;
he would be very much on the alert in the Washout,

although it seemed a bit ridiculous to think the un-savory bunch would attempt anything there.

"Tonight, you do exactly as I tell you, and when I tell you," he told the girl as they neared the lake-front place.

"Don't I always, dear?" she replied.

"Yes, guess you do," he admitted. "But things are rather rowdy tonight, don't forget that."

"I have nothing to fear when I'm with you," she replied.

"I appreciate your confidence in me," he smiled. "Hope it won't be misplaced."

"It won't be," she said confidently.

The Washout was lively, all right, whooping it up to a fare-you-well. Thankful Yates noticed their en-trance at once and came hurrying to greet them, the inevitable bottles under his arm.

"Felt sure you'd be along," he said. "Saved that little table over there not far from the door, where there's fresh air coming in—sorta foggy in here. Joyce Echols and a couple more of the boys are down at the other end of the bar. How are you, Miss Nor-man? Nice to see you again."

"And nice to see you, Mr. Yates," Jerry returned, extending her hand, over which Thankful bowed gallantly. He summoned a waiter to bring glasses.

"Your favorite wine, and my private bottle for Mr. Slade," he said as he filled the glasses to the brim.

As they sipped their drinks, Slade studied the crowd. There were a great many railroad workers, a fair sprinkling of cowhands, citizens from uptown, and quite a few others he recognized as lake-front habitués—about whom the less said the better—quite likely on the watch for the unwary with a snort too many under their belts. Robbing drunks and

pilfering wallets were some of the nice little prac-
tices they indulged in.

Gradually his attention focused on three men
standing at the end of the bar nearest the door, who
appeared to be absorbed in their drinks. They wore
the garb of railroad workers—overalls, jumpers, and
cloth caps. They did not seem to be mingling with
the others. He was about to pass them over as of no
consequence when his keen eyes noticed something
that instantly put him on the alert.

Showing under the sagging cuffs of the overalls
were not the laced, hobnailed shoes favored by the
railroad workers but *rangeland riding boots!*

After that, while chatting with Jerry, his eyes never
left the trio.

Young Joyce Echols came ambling over from the
bar. "Come on, Jerry, give me a dance," he requested.
"Walt won't mind, will you, Walt?"

"Certainly not," Slade replied. "Take her off my
hands for a spell—my ears are buzzing from her
chatter."

"I'll remember that, Mr. Slade, at just the right
time," she promised and headed for the dance floor,
Joyce's arm about her trim waist. Although not
seeming to do so, Slade's gaze concentrated on the
three men at the end of the bar. His hands rested on
the table top, his thumbs hooked under the edge.

Suddenly they whirled to face him, hands streak-
ing under their jumpers.

Over went the table, Slade behind it. Slugs ham-
mered at the top but failed to penetrate the thick oaken
boards. A bullet fanned his face. Another clipped a
lock of hair from the side of his head. He drew and
shot over the edge of the table, left and right, left and
right.

One of the killers crumpled up like a sack of old clothes. A second reeled slightly. Then he and his companion dashed for the door. Slade threw up his guns but was forced to hold his fire. For now there were men between him and the target, frightened men who had jumped up from their tables and were diving in every direction to get out of line with the flying lead. He leaped to his feet, charged toward the door, and was engulfed in the swirling crowd.

Thankful Yates came roaring forward, sawed-off shotgun in hand, and was also swallowed up. Slade untangled himself, righted the table, sat down and began rolling a cigarette with fingers that spilled not a crumb of tobacco.

Jerry was beside him. "Oh, darling, are you all right?" she gasped.

"Never felt better," he returned, touching a match to the brain tablet. "What did you do with Joyce?"

"She left me like a streak of goose grease in a hurry," panted that worthy as he ranged himself alongside Slade, gun in hand. "What in blazes happened?"

"Some gents just got a mite careless," Slade replied, puffing on his cigarette. Echols mouthed and stared. Slade rose, courteously pulled out a chair for Jerry and eased her, trembling, into it.

Thankful Yates finally won free and joined them, apparently oblivious to the uproar that was shaking the rafters and causing the hanging lamps to jump.

"Mr. Slade, how in blazes did you catch on so fast?" he demanded.

"Well," the Ranger replied dryly, "I did not recall ever before seeing railroad-track workers wearing spurred riding boots. Their disguise was pretty good except for that one little detail they overlooked. I'm afraid it brought one of them bad luck," he added, jerking his head to the figure sprawled on the floor.

"Well, I'll be —d-d-hanged!" sputtered Thankful and belatedly bellowed for order. The barkeepers and floor men were already uttering soothing yells, with little effect.

"Guess you'd better try and get word to the sheriff," Slade suggested. "He'll want to look things over."

Thankful bawled an order to a swamper. "And drag that carcass out of the way before somebody falls over it and gets hurt," he added. Jerry, who had recovered from her fright, giggled.

"I think Mr. Yates is wonderful," she said. "He has such a delicious sense of humor."

Slade thought that "macabre" was a more appropriate descriptive adjective but refrained from saying so.

Chapter Seventeen

The body was shoved against the wall to await the arrival of the sheriff. Gradually, order was restored. For a while the shooting was excitedly discussed and admiring glances cast at Slade. Soon, however, it was forgotten, for the drinks were good and strong, the eyes of the girls bright, and to these hardy men, death sudden and sharp was something too often met with to make other than a fleeting impression.

"And as usual, Shaw stayed in the background, nothing to tie him up with what was done," Slade remarked to Jerry, when they were alone. "I think I nicked one of the pair that got away. I'd hoped to overtake him and perhaps persuade him to do a little talking."

"I'm glad you didn't get a chance to," Jerry declared energetically.

"Might have been for the best," he admitted. "Would have been just like Shaw to be waiting across the street to take a shot at me if his killers failed up and I came out." Jerry shuddered.

At that moment the sheriff and old Keith came hurrying in, the latter looking decidedly worried. He breathed relief when he saw both Jerry and Slade were okay. Carter muttered things that were not fitting for a lady's ears. He immediately gave the body a careful once-over.

"Nope, never saw the sidewinder before," he replied

to Slade's questioning glance. "Well, looks like your luck is still holding."

"Luck!" Jerry exclaimed reprovingly. "It wasn't luck, it was just about the fastest thinking anyone ever heard tell of."

"Really it wasn't," Slade differed. "Those enterprising gents gave me all the time in the world to plan just what to do. And they made that one little slip, the sort of thing it seems the outlaw brand always does, sooner or later. I experienced something similar once before. As original a disguise I ever saw or heard about—a pair garbed in the robes of Brothers of a Mexican Religious Order. They, too, made the fatal slip of not synchronizing their footgear with the rest of their outfit. Anybody would have known they were up to something, after noticing riding boots instead of sandals."

"Uh-huh, anybody with eyes that miss nothing," the sheriff observed dryly. "The Mexicans have it right when they say the eye of El Halcon sees all."

Joyce Echols who had been fortifying himself at the bar came back.

"What you say, Jerry," he asked. "Shall we finish our dance? Maybe Walt won't start another ruckus and bust it up."

"I've still got the jitters, but perhaps this time I can fall over somebody else's feet for a change, instead of my own. All right, I'll chance it. Walt, please be good—for a change."

They sauntered off together, arm in arm. The sheriff turned to Slade.

"It seems to me," he remarked judiciously, "that Shaw's bunch is pretty well thinned out. What do you think?"

"I'm inclined to agree with you," Slade replied.

"That it is very likely the pair who escaped are the scrapings of the barrel."

Carter sat thoughtful for a moment, then added, "And do you think there's a chance the hellion might pull out? After all, he sure hasn't had much luck of late."

"Frankly, I'm afraid of just that," Slade conceded. "I still lean to the opinion that Shaw's main objective was the acquisition of John Fletcher's land, although I must admit it is really nothing but conjecture on my part and I could be altogether wrong. But if so, I also think that Shaw has seen the handwriting on the wall to the extent that he knows he can never hope to acquire the holding, and that it is quite likely he is planning to pull out. But I greatly fear he will not do so until he makes one more good haul. After that, if he manages to pull it off, I believe he and his two hellions will hie themselves to fresh pastures."

"And if they do, you'll go hunting for them, I suppose."

"Of course," Slade replied simply. "I am a Texas Ranger and Tobar Shaw has broken Texas law and it's up to me to see that he is brought to justice, one way or another.

"Only," he added with a wry smile, "the way things stand at present, I have nothing on the elusive Mr. Shaw that would hold up in court. I don't think I have ever contacted such a shadowy, self-effacing character as Tobar Shaw. I can just hope to catch him dead to rights, and so far I haven't had much luck in that direction."

"Just a matter of time," the sheriff predicted confidently.

"Yes, but time is running out," Slade countered. "Once again we've got to start hammering our brains in an endeavor to anticipate his move, and this time without a railroad paycar conveniently providing a logical target for an outlaw operation."

"Which nobody else even thought of," the sheriff observed dryly. "I'm just waiting till you hit the bull's-eye again. Only next time I hope you'll let me in on the fun."

"I fear our ideas as to what constitutes fun differ," Slade said smilingly.

"Nope," the sheriff declared emphatically. "You ain't happy unless you're mixed up in some sort of a ruckus and you might as well admit it. But what in the devil will that horned toad make a try for? Another herd of cows?"

"I'd say definitely not," Slade replied. "Unless we are making a bad mistake, he hasn't enough hands left to venture on a large-scale rustling chore, the only kind that would be worth his while. It will have to be something three desperate and competent men can handle."

"Plenty of things three sidewinders of that brand can put over," growled Carter. "Oh, the devil! my head's going 'round and 'round like a fool dog chasin' his tail; I need a snort. Waiter!"

The dance floor was less crowded now and Slade and Jerry enjoyed a couple of numbers together. Foremen were circulating among the railroaders, urging them to call it a night and get a little rest before work started. The majority took the hint and began filing out, singing and shouting. Soon the Washout was pretty well emptied save for some diehard cowhands and others who apparently had no homes. Thankful Yates began casting suggestive glances at the clock. Jerry also glanced at the clock, then at Slade, smiling and lifting her eyebrows.

"Well," said the sheriff, "looks like things are quieting down, and aside from your ruckus, Walt, no serious trouble I've heard about. The railroad fellers aren't quick on the trigger like the waddies and most of their arguments are shouting and waving paws. Not too bad for a payday bust. Got a notion we can call it a night before long."

"And I think Uncle Keith and the boys have about had their quota," Jerry observed. "Notice they're sort of looking sideways at their glasses, and that's always a good sign. Shall we go?"

"Guess we could do worse," Slade agreed.

"And if you don't mind, I'll walk with you, just in case," said Carter.

Although he thought there was little chance of more trouble, Slade did not decline the offer.

The afternoon was getting along the following day when Slade visited the sheriff's office. The old peace officer gestured to the body on the floor.

"Several barkeeps remembered seeing him around the lake front, usually with a couple more hellions," he said. "Quite likely the pair who got away last night, I'd say."

"Doubtless," Slade agreed. "Anything on him of significance?"

Carter shook his head. "Nothing but quite a passel of *dinero*," he replied. "You should get a percentage cut of all you've brought in for the county treasury. Old Potter County is getting rich, and she don't give a hang if it is blood money, as you might call it. Well, we can use the money and get along very well without that sort of blood."

Slade chuckled. The sheriff's sense of humor was a mite "blood-curdling," he thought.

For a while they smoked and talked and drank coffee, while the sun meandered westward.

"Still can't figure anything that vinegaroon might make a try for?" Carter asked.

This time Slade shook his head. "I'm sure up a stump, as the saying goes," he answered. "Well, maybe we'll get a break."

They were due to, in short order, one about as grisly as the sheriff's sense of humor.

A deputy dropped in, accepted an invitation to take a load off his feet and have some coffee.

"Saw John Fletcher and Si Unger, his range boss, about an hour back," he remarked conversationally. "They were just leaving town. Swivel-eye told me Fletcher picked up his mortgage money at the bank this morning—the money he figures to pay for a bunch of improved cows being driven in the next day or two. A hefty passel of *dinero*, I gathered."

Walt Slade was suddenly all attention. "And he was talking about it in the Trail End?" he asked.

"Guess he was," the deputy replied, "according to Swivel-eye."

For a moment Slade sat silent, then he abruptly rose to his feet.

"Come on, Brian," he said. "Hartley, you stay here against the chance we might send for you," he told the deputy.

"What in blazes?" demanded the bewildered sheriff, when they were outside.

"To the stable," Slade said. "Get the rig on your horse as fast as you can. I didn't tell Hartley to come along because his nag can't keep up with Shadow and your roan. I only hope we aren't too late."

"What do you mean?" asked Carter, still badly puzzled.

"I mean," Slade answered, "that I have a very strong feeling that Tobar Shaw is going to take advantage of an opportunity handed him on a silver platter, as it were."

"You figure he aims to make a try for Fletcher's money?"

"So I think," Slade said. "If we can catch up with Fletcher and Unger before they reach the Canadian Valley crossing, we may prevent it. At the crossing is very likely where the try will be made—no favorable spot between here and the crossing. If we aren't in time, I'm afraid Fletcher's and Unger's lives aren't worth a busted peso."

The sheriff swore luridly and saddled up with hot haste and they rode out of town.

Slade set the pace, gradually increasing their speed until the limit of Carter's tall roan was reached. For a moment he contemplated forging ahead, as Shadow could easily have done, but decided against it as being foolhardy. Odds of three, possibly more, to one, were just a mite lopsided and he had no way of knowing what he might be up against as he neared the crossing. And after all, their quarry having more than an hour's start, with Fletcher known as a rider with loose rein and busy spur, there was little hope of catching up before nearing the crossing. He glanced anxiously at the westering sun but concluded they should reach the descent into the Valley quite a while before dark.

Swiftly the miles flowed back under the horses' speeding hoofs. Slade kept gazing far ahead, toward where the curve of the horizon steadily advanced. Finally he sighted the fringe of growth along the Valley lip. A little more and he uttered a sharp exclamation.

"What is it?" Carter asked anxiously.

"Horses," Slade replied. "Two horses with empty hulls. Brian, it looks bad."

The sheriff gazed with squinted eyes. "I can see 'em now," he said, a moment later. "Grazing alongside the brush. Don't see hide or hair of the riders."

"And very likely you won't," Slade said grimly, and quickened the pace a little more, the roan laboring to keep up. And, in less than ten minutes, it was Carter who exclaimed.

"Do you see 'em?" he asked, his voice shaking. "Two bodies on the ground?"

"Yes, I see them," Slade answered quietly. "Looks like we're too late."

"My God! both done for!" Carter groaned. Slade nodded; it sure looked that way.

Chapter Eighteen

But as they thundered up to the brush, one of the "dead" men began to writhe and jerk. So did the other.

"Not dead, bound and gagged!" the Ranger cried. "What in blazes! Trail, Shadow, trail!"

Instantly the great black surged forward, leaving the roan as if it were standing still. Close to the neatly hogtied forms on the ground, Slade pulled him to a slithering halt and was out of the saddle with the horse still in motion. He knelt beside old John Fletcher, who mouthed and mumbled behind the handkerchief knotted over his mouth. Before the sheriff arrived on his blowing horse, Slade had the rancher freed of gag and cords and was working on Si Unger who, once the gag was out, cut loose with a flood of appalling profanity.

"Hold it!" El Halcon barked. "Tell us what happened."

"The blankety-blanks—three of 'em—caught us settin'!" bawled Fletcher, rubbing his numbed wrists. They ordered us out of our hulls and trussed us up—thought I was going to choke. Cleaned the saddle pouches and away they went—got every blankety-blank cent of my mortgage money. Had black rags over their faces."

"Which way did they go?" Slade asked. Fletcher gestured to the southeast.

"That way," he said.

"Walt, I betcha the hellions are headed for the railroad—going to catch a train and pull out," said Carter. "Maybe we can catch 'em up."

Slade silenced him with a gesture. "And you're positive they headed south by east, Mr. Fletcher?"

"Sure for certain," the rancher declared. "I could crane my neck up a bit and I watched 'em almost outa sight. They never swerved."

Slade turned to the sheriff. "Something very strange about this," he said. "Shaw is not in the habit of leaving witnesses alive. In my opinion, he spared Fletcher and Unger for a purpose, knowing they would note which way he went, to throw off possible pursuit."

"By gosh, I expect you're right," agreed the sheriff.

"Shaw!" repeated Fletcher, in an astonished voice. "You mean to say Shaw was one of those devils?"

"He was," Slade said tersely, and explained briefly why he believed so. Fletcher outdid Unger in swearing.

"Listen, Brian," Slade said, "we'll give the horses half an hour or so to graze a little and catch their breath, then I'm going to play a hunch. I believe it is a straight one, but if it isn't, I don't see that we have much to lose."

The sheriff understood at once. "Going to head west, eh?"

"That's right," Slade replied. "I'm of the opinion the hellions will head west across the desert and into New Mexico hill country till they decide on another area of operation. Mr. Fletcher, you and Si might as well go home, or back to Amarillo, whichever you prefer. I hope to recover your money for you, although I can't promise for sure."

"I've a darned good notion you'll do it," Fletcher said with confidence. "But why can't Si and me go along with you fellers? We might come in handy."

"Quite likely you would, but the trouble is you can't keep up with us," Slade vetoed the suggestion. "Shadow is in a class by himself and Brian's roan is mighty good. We'll be riding fast."

"I see," Fletcher conceded. "Well, good hunting! I guess Si and me will make for Amarillo and wait for you there."

With the bits flipped out and the cinches loosened, Shadow and the roan began putting away a surrounding of grass. Fletcher and Unger, whose cayuses were not in need of rest, elected to start for Amarillo without delay. Slade and the sheriff relaxing comfortably with cigarette and pipe, watched them grow small in the distance.

"Honestly, it wasn't so much that I was afraid their horses couldn't stand the pace, but I believe we can handle the chore more adequately by ourselves," Slade explained. "With a much better chance to work the element of surprise in our favor—a big advantage. We have a long and hard ride ahead of us, but our horses are in good shape and we won't push them at first. I feel confident that Shaw will stop at his ranchhouse to rest his mounts, or perhaps change them, and make ready for the trip across the desert. I figure we can cover a good part of the desert trek before the sun rises, which will help."

"You're aiming to cross the desert?" Carter asked.

"To that dry wash where the hidden water is," Slade replied. "They'll stop there, that's certain, and there is where we should be able to get the jump on them. It is highly doubtful that they will expect pursuit across the desert, and I am sure they won't suspect us of being holed up in the wash waiting for them to show."

"Sounds reasonable," the sheriff conceded. "Do you think Shaw finally caught on that you suspected him?"

"I've a notion he did," Slade said. "Anyhow, it's pretty sure he concluded the section had gotten a mite too hot and he'd do better to go on the hunt for fresh pastures.

"Getting back to Fletcher and Unger," he added with a chuckle, "there was an angle they in their excitement plumb overlooked."

"How's that?" Carter asked.

"That Shaw relieved them of their artillery before tieing them up," Slade answered. "Neither one had a gun."

"Dadgum it! Now that you mention it, you're right," snorted Carter. "Say, do you ever miss anything? I plumb overlooked it, too."

Slade laughed, and changed the subject. "I'm afraid we are going to do a little law-breaking on our own account," he said.

"How's that?"

"Little doubt but that dry wash is the other side of the New Mexico Territorial Line, where neither of us has any authority," Slade explained.

"I figure we're packing all we'll need," the sheriff said grimly, tapping his gun butt.

"I'm inclined to agree," Slade admitted. "Anyhow, the governor and Captain McNelty are pretty good friends, and I guess we can risk it. Well, our cayuses appear to have packed away their surrounding and are rarin' to go, so we might as well get moving."

It still lacked quite a while till sunset when they set

out, heading west by slightly south, on a long slant that Slade knew was the shortest line to the desert crossing. Riding at a good pace but not pushing their mounts, they covered mile after mile and as the dusk neared, Slade was quite pleased with their progress.

"Yes, we'll cover the major portion of the desert to the wash before the sun really begins to get in its licks," he told his companion. "And if the contrary desert just behaves itself and doesn't kick up another unexpected storm, we should do all right. It's a very uncertain terrain, however, and not to be depended on. Well, we'll have to do the best we can, no matter what happens."

"And that's all anybody can do," said Carter.

The stars blossomed in the blue-black vault of the sky and the great hush of the wastelands enfolded the two horsemen. It was an hour Slade loved, anywhere and under any circumstances, but he felt that on open range it was at its best, the hour when all things seemed relaxed, quiescent, building up strength for the activities to come. Soon the coyotes would begin their chorus, the owls their cheerful hooting, other night birds their weird cries. But now the stillness pressed down like something tangible, with breathless expectancy.

The miles flowed back, the hours passed, now attuned to the sprightly noises of the night. Slade veered the course a little more to the south, until they saw in the distance the star-drenched mystery of the desert.

"And now comes the real nice portion of our jaunt," he observed to Carter. "The real cosy angle is whether or not I made a mistake in assuming Shaw and his two horned toads will pause at the ranch-house for a while. If they did, okay. If they didn't, they're ahead of us, will reach the wash before we do and be all set to treat us as settin' quail, which is exactly what we will be, riding up to the wash in the open with the late moon or the early day providing good shooting light. In fact, I wish you'd let me handle this part alone."

"Oh, go set on a cactus spine," the old sheriff snorted. "Where you go, I go, and if we take the Big Jump it'll be together and we can start all over together. But I don't think we'll be taking it tonight. I feel sure you've figured things out just right and that those sidewinders are the ones who'll take the Big Jump, if they don't have sense enough to knuckle under when we brace 'em. Let's go. Not at all hot right now."

With which they entered the desert and rode steadily across the whispering sands, the hoofs of the horses kicking up little puffs of the alkali dust that glinted in the starlight.

Mile after mile they covered. Finally the stars turned from gold to silver, dwindled to needle points of steel piercing the blue-black robe of night. The "robe" grayed, the stars winked out, the east flushed scarlet and gold, the eerie hush enshrouded them. Another moment and the flaming beauty of the desert manifolded, and once again the great rim of the sun pushed above the horizon and almost at once the heat intensified, beating up from the sands.

From time to time, Slade glanced back the way they had come, but the flatness of the terrain and the shimmer of the rising heat made visibility poor. So far as he could see, the desert behind lay empty.

And now, no great distance ahead, he perceived the scattered straggle of mesquite which fringed the lip of the wash. It would seem that if they were ahead

of the outlaws, all was well; but there was no guar-
antee that they were. And the wash steadily drew
nearer.

It was a business to make the flesh crawl and the
backbone grow cold, riding in the glare of the sun-
light toward that ominous lip, from which at any
moment might come a blaze of gunfire. He strained
his eyes to probe the growth, cast a glance to the
south, and gave vent to an exasperated mutter.

Chapter Nineteen

"Now what?" Carter asked. Slade gestured south-ward. Once again the dust banners were streaming from the crests of the far distant dunes.

"Oh, just something else to complicate matters," the Ranger replied. "Down there another blasted dust storm is building up and heading this way." He studied the southwest for a moment.

"But it doesn't appear to be a big one," he added. "The farthest dunes aren't crested with those infernal dust streamers. Well, there is nothing we can do about that." He turned and concentrated on the strag-gle of brush that seemed to leap toward them.

The distance shrank to five hundred yards, to four-fifty, to four, to three-fifty. Perfect rifle range. The situation was hard on even the steely nerves of El Halcon. He abruptly realized he was holding his breath, and exhaled it angrily. Three hundred! The tension eased a little. Another hundred yards dwin-dled away. Slade glanced at his companion. The sheriff's face was gray and drawn, his lips a straight line, but he glared straight ahead and drew his rifle from the saddle boot. Slade felt a surge of admira-tion for the old fellow. He was scared, no doubt as to that, but he wasn't going to falter.

And now El Halcon was breathing much easier; had something been going to happen, it should have happened before now. Just the same he heaved a sigh of relief as they charged up to the lip of the wash with the silence broken only by the thud of their horses' hoofs. If the hellions were holed up under one of the overhangs, they were certainly not aware of the pursuers' approach. Now the odds were more like even. He sent Shadow surging down the slope. A quick glance showed them the wash was devoid of life.

"Well, we made it," he added as Carter drew rein beside him. "Now the advantage should be ours. That is if my hunch is a straight one and the devils are really headed this way. And if that dust storm will just slow up a bit we should make out all right. We'll shelter the horses under that wide overhang and give them some water from the canteens; beginning to get darn hot. Then we'll hole up in the shade for a bit. Nothing in sight so far, although I've a notion if they really are going to show it will be before long."

Carter chuckled creakily. "Riding up to this crack, I forgot all about the heat," he said. "Reckon my blood was running sorta cold."

"I could have been more comfortable myself," Slade admitted. "It was a ticklish business. Now we might as well take it easy for a spell."

Sitting down in the shade, he rolled a cigarette and smoked with enjoyment. From time to time he climbed the slope to peer over the edge. At the fourth trip he uttered an exultant exclamation.

"They're coming, all three of them," he told his companion. "Less than a mile away. Get set. I don't think they'll be taken without a fight, but we've got to give them a chance to surrender."

Tense and alert, they waited. Finally Slade heard the slithering thud of hoof beats on the sands. Another moment and two riders came skating down the slope and into plain view. Slade's voice rang out—

"Up! You're covered!"

The startled horses reared. Yelling a volley of oaths, the two riders went for their holsters. The slopes of the wash quivered to the roar of gunfire.

But the advantage was with the men on foot. Shooting with both hands, Slade saw one of the riders pitch out of his saddle. The sheriff's Colt boomed twice and the second man fell, to lie motionless. With a whoop of victory, Carter started forward.

"Look out!" Slade roared. "There's another one. It must be Shaw." The sheriff cursed luridly and dived for safety.

Keeping as much under cover as possible, Slade never took his eyes off the brush-fringed crest, from which came no sound or movement.

"If he's holed up in the bush, smoking him out is going to be a chore," he muttered.

Minutes passed, and nothing happened. Nerves were stretched to the breaking point. Then suddenly Carter let out a yelp.

"There he goes!" he bawled. "Look! There he goes!"

Slade whirled to glance toward where the sheriff pointed. Fully a mile to the south, a horseman rode down the near slope, sped across the floor, and up the far side to vanish over the crest. Slade ran to where Shadow stood, flipped in the bit and mounted.

"You all right?" he asked anxiously, for Carter was swabbing at a blood-streaming face.

"I'm okay," the sheriff answered. "Get the blankety-blank; I'll be following you. Those hellions on the ground are done for."

"I'll get him," Slade said. "He's not going to out-run old Shadow."

But the moment he topped the slope, he realized it would be a long and hard chase. Shaw was well mounted, and now he had nearly two miles start and was heading straight for the hills. Slade settled himself in the saddle and gave Shadow his head. At the same time he glanced anxiously to the south and saw what might well make his best effort hopeless. The tall dunes had vanished from view and as he saw it once before, the vague, purplish curtain was sweeping steadily north. He urged Shadow to greater speed.

The great black responded gallantly and steadily closed the gap. But that ominous cloud in the south advanced even faster.

Mile after mile, through the searing heat! Shadow's nostrils were flaring, his eyes gorged with blood, but he never faltered, and slowly, slowly closed the distance.

But now the hills loomed close, and the quarry was still half a mile and more in the lead, and nearer, nearer was the vanguard of the storm. Slade fingered the butt of his Winchester, but shook his head. The distance was too great; a hit would be just a fluke.

"A little more, feller, just a little more!" he begged. And Shadow came across. Slade drew the Winchester from the boot.

So intent was he on his quarry that he forgot the storm, and his pulses actually skipped a beat when suddenly Shaw vanished as if plucked from the earth by a magic hand. Another instant and he, too, was enveloped.

Again the bellowing wind! Again the flying yellow shadows, again the searing heat and the blinding dust. Shadow sneezed and coughed. Slade whipped his neckerchief over his nose and mouth and leaned forward in the saddle.

"This'll be a short one, feller, just a squall," he gasped. "Not like that other. Keep going, horse, we've got to make the hills."

Doggedly, Shadow slogged forward, coughing and sneezing, blowing hard, but making steady progress. Slade calculated the distance to the sanctuary they sought; he believed they'd be able to make it. Must be close now. And this shouldn't last long.

It didn't, although it seemed an eternity of discomfort and unease. As suddenly as it struck, the storm passed. The air cleared, the sun shone down. Slade glanced forward eagerly. The hills were only a few hundred yards distant; but the desert stretched lonely and deserted. He muttered a bitter oath. Under cover of the storm, Shaw had made good his escape. He had reached the hills before his pursuer and to attempt to track him through that maze of canyons and gorges would be rank nonsense. Tobar Shaw was still unfinished business.

Well, he had experienced such a situation before and things had eventually worked out, so what the devil! He turned and gazed back the way he had come. Far in the distance he could make out a bouncing blob steadily drawing nearer. The old sheriff was gamely following on his trail. He halted Shadow, who snorted disgustedly, waited a little, then waved a reassuring hand. Carter, understanding, eased up on his laboring mount. Before long he drew rein beside El Halcon, his horse pretty groggy but still able to navigate.

"Got away," Slade answered his panted question. "Storm hid him for long enough to make the hills. No use swearing about it, just one of those things.

Come on, we've got to find some shade before we bake."

As they rode on, he added, "Yes, he got in the clear, and do you realize that we still haven't a thing on the cunning devil? He could walk into the Trail End tomorrow, sit down and grin at us. Never have we spotted him in some off-color business, and all those who could testify against him are dead. And today I didn't get close enough to be able to swear the man I pursued was Shaw. He's the limit! This last caper of his was true to form. Always farsighted, he let his two hands ride into the wash while he stayed on top—may have somehow suspected something. Under cover of the shooting, he sent his horse skalleyhooting to the south, crossed the wash and headed for the hills. And with the help of that blasted dust storm he made it. Oh, well, perhaps next time. Sure he'll come back to Texas; I'm convinced of that, and start operating in an entirely different role, the chances are. His sort never quits."

"Neither do the Rangers," growled Carter. "Still just a matter of time. Say, that crack ahead looks pretty good."

A few minutes later they entered a narrow canyon which bored westward into the hills and rode in the grateful shade of an overhanging wall.

"I've a notion we should find water in here," Slade remarked.

They did, a little spring bubbling from under a cliff. As usual, Slade had some staple provisions in the pouches and they kindled a fire and shortly enjoyed an appetizing meal with plenty of steaming coffee to wash it down, while the horses made out very well with a small helping of oats and the sparse grass that grew on the canyon floor. After which men and critters rested in the shade for a couple of hours. Slade patched up the sheriff's bullet-gashed cheek, the wound being slight.

"Now I figure we can risk heading for the wash," he said. "Don't appear to be any more storms in the making and I think we can do it by dark."

It was a hard drag, but they made it without mishap. They had refilled their canteens from the spring and there was water for the horses.

While resting again, they examined the saddle pouches of the dead outlaws' mounts and drew forth packets of bills which the sheriff counted with satisfaction.

"Looks like we got back most of Fletcher's *dinero*," he observed.

"Yes, about two-thirds, I'd say," Slade replied. "They must have divided the money before they started out. Shaw will be packing the other third and be well heeled to head for wherever he is of a notion to."

"Hope the sidewinder chokes on it," growled Carter.

"Perhaps he will," Slade smiled. "Another couple of hours rest and we should be able to make the remainder of the crossing without trouble in the cool of the night, even though the cayuses are pretty well fagged. Then another short halt and we'll head for Keith Norman's casa, which isn't so far off from the other side of the desert. Guess we can take along the carcasses. The horses they rode appear to be in good shape."

"And then?"

"And then after a couple of days at Norman's place to rest, I'll be heading back to the Post to see what Captain Jim has lined up for me," Slade replied.

It was long past daylight when they reached the XT

ranchhouse and after one look at them, Jerry packed them both off to bed. Two days later, she said gaily to Slade—"Well, good hunting at your next stop!" But as she watched him ride away to where duty called and new adventure waited, her eyes were wistful.

Bradford Scott was a pseudonym for **Leslie Scott** who was born in Lewisburg, West Virginia. During the Great War, he joined the French Foreign Legion and spent four years in the trenches. In the 1920s he worked as a mining engineer and bridge builder in the western American states and in China before settling in New York. A bar-room discussion in 1934 with Leo Margulies, who was managing editor for Standard Magazines, prompted Scott to try writing fiction. He went on to create two of the most notable series characters in Western pulp magazines. In 1936, Standard Magazines launched, and in *Texas Rangers*, Scott under the house name of **Jackson Cole** created Jim Hatfield, Texas Ranger, a character whose popularity was so great with readers that this magazine featuring his adventures lasted until 1958. When others eventually began contributing Jim Hatfield stories, Scott created another Texas Ranger hero, Walt Slade, better known as *El Halcon*, the Hawk, whose exploits were regularly featured in *Thrilling Western*. In the 1950s Scott moved quickly into writing book-length adventures about both Jim Hatfield and Walt Slade in long series of original paperback Westerns. At the same time, however, Scott was also doing some of his best work in hardcover Westerns published by Arcadia House; thoughtful, well-constructed stories, with engaging characters and authentic settings and situations. Among the best of these, surely, are *Silver City* (1953), *Longhorn Empire* (1954), *The Trail Builders* (1956), and *Blood on the Rio Grande* (1959). In these hardcover Westerns, many of which have never been reprinted, Scott proved himself highly capable of writing traditional Western stories with characters who have sufficient depth to change in the course of the narrative and with a degree of authenticity and historical accuracy absent from many of his series stories.

INTERACT WITH DORCHESTER ONLINE!

Want to learn more about your favorite books and authors?
Want to talk with other readers that like to read the same books as you?
Want to see up-to-the-minute Dorchester news?

VISIT DORCHESTER AT:
DorchesterPub.com
Twitter.com/DorchesterPub
Facebook.com (Search Pages)

DISCUSS DORCHESTER'S NOVELS AT:
Dorchester Forums at DorchesterPub.com
GoodReads.com
LibraryThing.com
Myspace.com/books
Shelfari.com
WeRead.com

Johnny D. Boggs
Killstraight

"A rousing story with an emotional and philosophical depth."
—*Booklist*

CULTURE CLASH

Daniel Killstraight is on his way back to the Comanche reservation after spending seven years learning the ways of whites at a special school back East. But he's met with a grisly homecoming: the hanging of his childhood friend Jimmy Comes Last for a horrific double murder. When asked by his old friend's mother to prove that her dead son was innocent, Daniel can't say no.

Caught between two worlds, Daniel struggles to carve out a place for himself and track down the truth. Reluctantly, he joins the tribal Indian Police and soon begins to believe that Jimmy's mother was right, that her son wasn't guilty. As he digs further into the crime, he uncovers something much bigger than murder ...

"The relationships and setting shine: Daniel—striving at once to solve the case and reconnect with Comanche ways—is a complex, winning protagonist." —*Publishers Weekly*

ISBN 13: 978-0-8439-6307-6

Bill Pronzini &
Marcia Muller

The dark clouds are gathering, and it's promising to be a doozy of a storm at the River Bend stage station ... where the owners are anxiously awaiting the return of their missing daughter. Where a young cowboy hopes to find safety from the rancher whose wife he's run away with. Where a Pinkerton agent has tracked the quarry he's been chasing for years. Thunder won't be the only thing exploding along ...

CRUCIFIXION RIVER

Bill Pronzini and Marcia Muller are a husband-wife writing team with numerous individual honors, including the Lifetime Achievement Award from the Private Eye Writers of America, the Grand Master Award from Mystery Writers of America, and the American Mystery Award. In addition to the Spur Award–winning title novella, this volume also contains stories featuring Bill Pronzini's famous "Nameless Detective" and Marcia Muller's highly popular Sharon McCone investigator.

ISBN 13: 978-0-8439-6341-0

The Classic Film Collection

The Searchers by Alan LeMay

Hailed as one of the greatest American films, *The Searchers*, directed by John Ford and starring John Wayne, has had a direct influence on the works of Martin Scorsese, Steven Spielberg, and many others. Its gorgeous cinematic scope and deeply nuanced characters have proven timeless. And now available for the first time in decades is the powerful novel that inspired this iconic movie.

Destry Rides Again by Max Brand

Made in 1939, the Golden Year of Hollywood, *Destry Rides Again* helped launch Jimmy Stewart's career and made Marlene Dietrich an American icon. Now available for the first time in decades is the novel that inspired this much-loved movie.

The Man from Laramie by T. T. Flynn

In its original publication, *The Man from Laramie* had more than half a million copies in print. Shortly thereafter, it became one of the most recognized of the Anthony Mann/Jimmy Stewart collaborations, known for darker films with morally complex characters. Now the novel upon which this classic movie was based is once again available—for the first time in more than fifty years.

The Unforgiven by Alan LeMay

In this epic American novel, which served as the basis for the classic film directed by John Huston and starring Burt Lancaster and Audrey Hepburn, a family is torn apart when an old enemy starts a vicious rumor that sets the range aflame. Don't miss the powerful novel that inspired the film the *Motion Picture Herald* calls "an absorbing and compelling drama of epic proportions."

☐ **YES!**

Sign me up for the Leisure Western Book Club and send my FREE BOOKS! If I choose to stay in the club, I will pay only $14.00* each month, a savings of $9.96!

NAME: _____

ADDRESS: _____

TELEPHONE: _____

EMAIL: _____

☐ I want to pay by credit card.

☐ **VISA**   ☐ **MasterCard.**   ☐ **DISCOVER**

ACCOUNT #: _____

EXPIRATION DATE: _____

SIGNATURE: _____

Mail this page along with $2.00 shipping and handling to:
Leisure Western Book Club
PO Box 6640
Wayne, PA 19087
Or fax (must include credit card information) to:
610-995-9274

You can also sign up online at **www.dorchesterpub.com.**
*Plus $2.00 for shipping. Offer open to residents of the U.S. and Canada only.
Canadian residents please call 1-800-481-9191 for pricing information.
If under 18, a parent or guardian must sign. Terms, prices and conditions subject to change. Subscription subject to acceptance. Dorchester Publishing reserves the right to reject any order or cancel any subscription.